What I Learned That Summer

BRANDI EASTERLING COLLINS

LUMINESCE
•PUBLISHING•

Luminesce Publishing books may be ordered
through booksellers or by contacting:

Luminesce Publishing
www.luminescepublishing.com

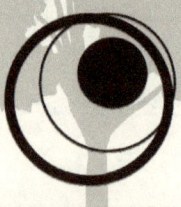

LUMINESCE
•PUBLISHING•

Cover image © Brandi Easterling Collins
Illustrations designed by Freepik
Cover design © Luminesce Publishing
Interior design © Luminesce Publishing
Author photos © Felisha Weaver Photography

ISBN: 978-1-7322289-4-8 (paperback)
ISBN: 978-1-7322289-5-5 (ebook)

Library of Congress Control Number: 2019911081

Acknowledgements:

Thank you to my husband, Jonathan, for being supportive of my dreams and offering opinions from a male perspective when needed. Thank you to my children, Drew and Meredith, for allowing me time to write and read.

Thank you to my wonderful friends and beta readers, Alisha, Devin, Felisha, Melissa, and Sarah for their valuable feedback and support of this story.

Thank you to Felisha Weaver for photography and graphic design consultation.

Thank you for the continued support of the Campbell, Collins, Easterling, and Russell families.

Special thanks to authors Devin Cutting and Sarah Krewis for being excellent friends and critique partners. Thank you to the #amwriting, #writingcommunity, and #IndieFeature Twitter communities for the continuous support and encouragement of independent authors.

Thank you to my two favorite mutts, Buddy and Peanut, for being a captive audience during my read-aloud editing sessions.

This novel is dedicated to my aunt,
Diana Lynn Russell Fleming,
who left this world in 2018.

Book Dedication

To my Aunt, Diana Fleming.
For buying me a 25¢ bag
of Cheetos at the Downtown (Benton)
Harvest Foods on April 13, 1996.
(saturday) at 9:05 p.m.
    And I promised her that
when I became a writer, I
would dedicate one of my
books to her for that reason.

Chapter 1
Monday, June 12, 1995

From what I'd seen, movies that featured motels by lakes never ended well. But it didn't surprise me that my parents never asked me if I wanted to stay here for the summer; they just threw a duffel bag at me and told me to pack enough stuff for eight weeks. Two months away from my friends, practically stranded in the middle of nowhere with my grandparents at their small motel.

Dad pulled into the motel parking lot and braked hard enough to jolt me from my thoughts.

"Kincaid," my mother said. "Get your bags."

"Mom," I said. "I'm too old for a babysitter. Can't I just stay at home?"

"A fifteen-year-old girl, especially one with your history, has no business staying alone for the summer," my father said, the word "history" spewing from his mouth like snake venom. "You're staying here. Get your butt out of the car."

I relented and grabbed my lightest two bags from the trunk as my parents disappeared into the main office to talk to my grandparents. I'd last visited the motel when I was eleven, back when it was fun and only for a few days at a time—a week at the most. "Ugh, the smell," I muttered. "This whole place stinks like fish guts and old people."

"That's part of its charm," a male voice said from behind me. "You get used to it."

I jumped and turned around. A suntanned, shirtless boy about my age stood in front of me. "You almost gave me a heart attack!"

"You look a bit young for a heart attack," he said, pushing his dark hair off his forehead. "Probably almost wet your pants, though. I'm Joseph. You must be Kincaid."

I looked over the top of my sunglasses. "You really shouldn't sneak up on people like that," I growled at him.

"You're just as delightful as your grandparents said," Joseph said dryly. He picked up my heaviest bag out of the trunk as if it weighed nothing and placed it on the sidewalk. "And I didn't sneak up on you. I've been hanging around here the whole time just minding my own business until you came and started complaining in my space."

He had a point. I'd been so distracted by the stench I hadn't looked behind me. "And why would you want to hang around this place?"

"That's easy. They pay me and my sister to be here."

"Your sister?"

"I think she's cleaning one of the vacant guest rooms. Her name's Veronica. She's working as a maid with your aunt Sylvia."

Another girl to talk to, thank goodness. And she had an awesome first name—the same as the lead character in *Heathers*, one of my favorite movies. "Sounds like they won't even need me to work." I sighed with relief. "They couldn't possibly need anyone else." There were only twenty rooms.

"Nope. But you won't get to sit around doing nothing. Your grandpa wouldn't hear of it. He's already asked me to take you under my wing."

"Really?" He couldn't possibly be much older than me, and now he was my unofficial boss for the summer? "How old are you, anyway?"

"Old enough to put in a hard day's work," he said with a sly grin. "But for argument's sake, let's say I'm able to drive with a hardship license because I'm not old enough for a real one."

"Fifteen?"

"Yeah."

"Me too."

"I know," he said. "Your grandparents told me all about you...except for the pink hair. I expected you to be as pretty as the photo they showed me, but I didn't think you'd look like a clown college dropout."

"Do you think you're funny?" I crossed my arms. Did everyone have to make a comment? My parents hadn't said a word about it—much to my surprise. "It washes out, you know."

"No. They don't pay me to be funny. They pay me because I'm handy with a hammer and a bucket of paint."

"Well, I'm not good with manual labor."

"Don't worry, princess," he said, taking my hand. He pointed to my nail polish. "I'll show you. If you can paint a fingernail, you can paint a fence post."

"Kincaid!" my mother called from my grandparents' door. "Come on in here for a minute so we can say goodbye."

Joseph watched as my mom went back inside.

"I better go," I told him.

"I'll see you later. Nice meeting you, Kincaid."

"Yeah," I said as I walked away.

3

"Chester, Darla," my father said to my grandparents. "Call me if Kincaid gives you any trouble. We've warned her not to do anything stupid like she did back home."

I groaned. I'd hoped my parents wouldn't tell anyone about my incident since I hadn't actually done anything wrong. But just being there with my boyfriend had gotten me into trouble, too, although the charges had been dropped. Who was I kidding? He wasn't really my boyfriend. He'd only kissed me once the same day we were arrested, and I'd only had, like, five significant conversations with him my whole life. We'd never even hung out until the week of spring break when all our friends were out of town.

Grandma placed her hands on her hips. "Kincaid's a good girl, Daniel," she said.

"Someone forgot to tell her that," Dad said. He hugged me briefly, kissed the top of my head, his anger burning through like poison, and then he walked out to the car.

My mother turned to me. "No talking to Derek," she said. "I mean it."

"He stopped talking to me after Dad yelled at him and called him a loser," I grumbled. "He doesn't even know I'm here." In reality, he probably didn't care either. I was working on accepting that.

"You're too young for a boyfriend anyway," Mom said, removing my sunglasses. "Please try to have a good summer. Being away from everything will do you good. Sit by the lake, enjoy the sunsets, and read some good books from the library. You might even learn a thing or two." She pulled me into her arms and hugged me until

I couldn't breathe. "I'm doing this for you," she whispered into my ear.

I pulled out of my mother's grip and watched her hug my grandparents. Mom hung her head as she pulled away.

"Susan," Grandma said quietly. "You know, you can always come back here."

Mom shushed Grandma and then glanced at me. "Everything's going to be fine, Mom. I'll call you when we get settled." The horn blared from outside, and Mom gave me one last pathetic smile before she ran outside and got in the car.

I turned to my grandparents, who were grinning wildly at me, and sighed. Things were so much easier when I was six. Then, all they had to do was fill me up with sodas and candy to make me forget my worries.

Joseph was just dropping my bags off in my room as Grandpa led me through the attached door from their living room. Room one was their permanent guest room. "Thank you, Joe," he said. "Have you met my beautiful granddaughter?"

He grinned at me. "Yes, Mr. Kincaid," he said. "I've met the namesake you've told me so much about."

"Please show her around," Grandpa said. "She hasn't seen the improvements over the last two years, and I think she'll be quite impressed." He left me alone with the shirtless boy.

"Do you want to change shoes first?" Joseph pointed to my feet.

Still irritated that he'd called me "princess" earlier, I crossed my arms and popped both ankles inside my platform sandals. "I'll be fine. Let's get this over with."

Joseph showed me an unpainted wood fence around what my grandparents called "the playground" which was really just a metal swing-set, a few picnic tables, and a couple of grills on poles. "You'll be helping me paint the fence starting tomorrow," he said with a warm smile.

"Can't wait!" I exclaimed with all the fake enthusiasm I could manage.

He turned to me, no longer smiling, and crossed his arms. "Look, I'm sorry your parents forced you to be here, but the least you can do is make the best of it. This is my summer, too, and I don't want to spend it babysitting you and your bad attitude."

What a jerk! "I'm sure your parents forced you and your sister to work here too," I said. "This place isn't all that glamorous. It's the lake; it's not like it's the ocean."

Joseph shook his head. "Our parents don't force us to do anything," he said, spitting out his words as though they tasted bad. "Not anymore. Me and Veronica have already figured out the world doesn't revolve around us, and it doesn't owe us any favors. Maybe you'll learn that someday too." He walked away, toward the lake. "Come with me if you want to see the unglamorous lake and the stupid new dock."

Had he just called me a spoiled brat? I'd show him. He didn't know me at all. I ran to catch up with him and still had to force myself to walk faster than I normally would to keep up with his long legs. We stopped near the water as he pointed at the dock without saying a word to me.

6

My heart skipped a beat when I saw the blond god of a guy sitting at the top of the lifeguard stand.

My mouth dropped open. "Oh, my God," I whispered. He looked like one of the tanned beach bodies on one of my favorite television shows, *Beverly Hills, 90210,* where the two main characters shared my last name. I always imagined myself being their little sister, hanging out on the beach all the time.

"That's Todd," Joseph said.

Todd—it even rhymed with god. He climbed down from the stand and blew a whistle at some kids who had drifted out too far on their inflatable rafts. "Reel it back in, kids!" he called. He walked over to me. "Hey, you must be Kincaid. Your grandma was so excited to hear you'd be staying."

Oh, my God, breathe. "Yes," I said, finding my voice. "Kincaid Walsh. I'm thrilled to be here to help them out."

Joseph snickered. "I have to finish showing her around," he said. "See you later."

"Veronica working today, Joe?" Todd asked.

"She's cleaning today," Joseph said.

"Cool," Todd said as he walked away. I watched his every move.

Joseph looked at me and rolled his eyes. "I'm pretty sure my sister's staked her claim on him. Don't waste your time. He's too old for you, anyway." He walked away fast, and I struggled to catch up with him again. Just as I matched his stride, I stumbled over a rock by the bank and almost fell into the lake. Joseph caught me by the arms and laughed while he hoisted me back upright. "This is going to be fun, princess."

He stayed in my face longer than he had to. He thought he was cute, but he was dead wrong.

Chapter 2

The large picture window helped brighten up the dark paneling on the walls of my new home for the summer. Everything inside the room smelled damp and fishy like the air outside. The bedspread was a colorful handmade quilt with little girls in bonnets stitched all over it—the same one I used when I visited Grandma's house as a little girl, right before they bought the motel.

I worked on unpacking my bags, and Grandma joined me a few minutes later. "About done in here?" she asked.

"Yeah, almost," I said. "Does the phone in here work?"

"It does for local calls. For long-distance, you'll have to use the calling card I bought for you. Four hundred minutes."

"Thanks, Grandma." I sat on the bed. "And thanks for putting my favorite quilt in here."

She sat beside me and put her arm around me. "Are you still that sweet little snaggle-toothed girl who used to bake cookies with me? Because some of the things your mother told me were shocking. That's not my Kincaid."

It was disheartening having Grandma disappointed in me. She'd always defended me and called me 'spirited' when I got too rambunctious as a kid. Now, the way she looked at me made me want to cry. "I think so," I said, looking down at my hands. "They wouldn't even let me explain."

"Explain it to me, then. Tell me how my sweet Kincaid got arrested for shoplifting. I know I raised Susan better than that, and I know she raised you better than that too. 'Thou shalt not steal.'"

Crap, now she was quoting the Bible. "Technically, I didn't," I said as tears welled up in my eyes. "Derek stole, but I didn't know he was going to. He asked me to stand outside the store and wait for him, and because we'd been hanging out all week, I didn't think anything of it. He was gone just a couple of minutes, then he came out really fast, kissed me on the cheek, and took off running. The store owner chased him down, and then the police came. I was so scared; I didn't know what to do. They all assumed I was with him."

Derek had moved to my school halfway through tenth grade. His bright blond hair was grown out just enough to show his dark roots. From a distance, he was mysterious and attractive—like a young Kurt Cobain, whose death I'd only recently accepted. Everything about Derek intrigued me. He arrived at school every day carrying a skateboard on his shoulder. Right before the final bell would ring, he'd ride it all the way to his locker and throw it inside. I had the perfect view from my seat in homeroom.

From afar, I'd watched him for weeks until I finally had the courage to walk up and introduce myself right at the start of spring break. And what did he say to me? "Kincaid? What a weird-ass name," he'd said as he walked away. I wanted to talk to him even more after that, but he barely acknowledged me until the week we got in trouble. *What had I done wrong? Why did he do that to me?*

"Well, you were with him," Grandma said, throwing me back into the present. "You can't go around kissing frogs expecting one of them to turn into a prince. Think about the company you keep. When your friends are stealing cigarettes, you might as well be stealing them too."

"They told you about the cigarettes?"

"They told me, but I wanted to hear it from you. Did you smoke with that boy—the Derek character who stole cigarettes at fifteen years old?"

It sounded so much worse when an elderly lady scolded me. "No, I swear, I never smoked. Derek threw some to me before he ran off."

"They're bad for you. We know all this stuff now. Everyone smoked when I was your age, and I had a terrible time quitting when your uncle Ches was a baby. I don't want to see you hooked on those cancer sticks."

Grandpa walked in. "Cancer sticks? You better not be smoking."

"My friend did, not me," I said. "I won't do it."

"Your friends smoke—you smoke," Grandpa said as he cupped my chin. "You run around with barnyard animals; you're gonna wind up smelling like shit. Your slate's wiped clean here with us. Don't mess it up." He walked outside and called for Joseph.

Grandma stood up slowly and held her knee for a moment. "This getting old ain't for the weak," she said. "Finish unpacking and come help me with dinner at five. We're hosting everyone tonight to welcome you."

"Everyone?"

"Joe and Veronica, Sylvia...Todd —the lifeguard—I wasn't sure if you met him during the tour."

Todd. *Todd the god* was coming to dinner. I doubted I'd be able to chew. "Is Aunt Sylvia bringing Dane?" My cousin, Dane, had just graduated high school. Sylvia was only eighteen when he was born, barely out of high school herself.

"Nope. He's working up north and taking some college classes this summer. Just missed him by a couple of days."

After Grandma left, I stretched out on the bed to rest. I flipped on the television and scrolled through the cable channels, finally settling on MTV. Maybe having my own motel room wouldn't be so bad.

Light knocking on the external door woke me. I hadn't realized I was tired enough to fall asleep since I'd napped on and off during the drive, the mixed tapes in my Walkman my only company. I opened the door to find my aunt standing there grinning as much as her tiny mouth would allow. I fell into her arms. "Aunt Sylvia!"

"Kaykay!" she exclaimed, using my childhood nickname as she hugged me. "How are you, girl? And how'd you get to be so tall?" The top of her head landed just under my chin, her wiry blond hair tickling me as she moved.

"I don't know. It just happened, and some of it's my shoes. How are you?"

"The same. I was thrilled when I found out you'd be here for the summer. I've missed my girl! I didn't believe a word Susan said about you getting in trouble."

Geez, did everyone know? "I'm only here for eight weeks."

"That's practically the whole summer in teenage years. I gotta get back to helping Veronica. I'll see you at dinner, and we'll catch up."

12

I loved Sylvia. She was the best aunt. The last time I visited my grandparents, she'd taken me to see a movie and spent most of the day shopping with me while the motel underwent an inspection. Sylvia treated me like a teenager, which at eleven, was the thing I wanted most. She talked to me like I was already grown up. Thanks to her, I was prepared when I got my first period a year later, even though my mother wasn't.

Mom refused to acknowledge I was growing up. She didn't understand me at all. Not that Dad did, either. Since I'd gotten boobs, Dad barely looked at me. Sure, he'd gripe at me about my "C" in science (I planned to be a writer; who needed science anyway?) but barely acknowledged my poem that got picked up in the school newspaper. He'd yelled at me a lot after the shoplifting arrest but then stopped talking to me altogether.

Since my nap had been interrupted, I dragged my remaining bags to the bed and finished unpacking. I had no choice but to make the room my own for the next eight weeks.

Chapter 3

The aroma of Grandma's fried chicken made my mouth water and could put a Kentucky Fried Chicken restaurant to shame. It was what she'd always made for me when I visited when I was little. She'd take the whole chicken and cut up the pieces herself to save money. She never wasted anything. The first and only spanking I remembered getting from her was after I'd thrown away a half-eaten popsicle. I couldn't have been more than five at the time. Mom told me it was because Grandma was a child during the Great Depression, and sometimes she only had popcorn and applesauce to eat. I couldn't imagine that, but I'd never thrown away food in her presence again.

The kitchen cabinets were overflowing with Grandma's treasures for a rainy day: old bread bags, discarded cotton from medicine bottles, scrap balls of aluminum foil, rubber bands, twist-ties, fast-food napkins, and washed sandwich baggies. Each cabinet I opened threatened an avalanche of junk I didn't see the use of saving.

"Careful, Kincaid," she said. "I've always been a packrat."

"It's okay, Grandma. I just wanted to help you set the table. I thought the plates were over here last time."

She handed me a stack of plates from the dishrack. "We use them so much they're either in the sink or in the dishrack. It's just a waste of time to put them away." Mom would never hear of that. She would grab a plate out of my hands and wash it to avoid it being stacked in the sink.

I took the plates and began setting the table for the seven of us. I hoped Todd would sit across from me so I could look at him. I didn't care where Joseph sat but was looking forward to meeting his sister, Veronica. Aunt Sylvia and I would have tons of time to catch up over the summer.

Joseph and Veronica rang the doorbell at promptly seven o'clock. Grandpa let them in and shuffled them to the large eat-in kitchen. The place reminded me of a community center kitchen with a long farmer's table in the middle of the room, enclosed by the L-shaped counter and wall-to-wall cabinets surrounding everything.

Veronica was a petite brunette with short, spiky hair, better suited to be dressed in black leather than the pink baby doll dress she wore. "Kincaid!" she said as she walked over to me. She picked up a strand of my hair, revealing a massive scar on her arm. "Pink! I knew you'd be cool. Good to meet you, girl. Sorry you're stuck working with my squirt little brother." Joseph rolled his eyes and washed his hands in the kitchen sink. Veronica went to a drawer near the sink and pulled out cloth napkins for the table. She seemed to know her way around the kitchen better than Grandpa. "Maybe you can help me and Sylvia sometime."

"That'd be great. Nice to meet you too."

Sylvia arrived next, and Todd walked in right behind her. He was even hotter wearing a tight white t-shirt than he was with no shirt earlier. He smiled at me and joined Joseph and Veronica at the table. Sylvia and I helped Grandma put out the food. The heavenly scent made my stomach rumble as I looked at everyone. It was the strangest group I could imagine: three teenagers without their parents, my aunt—the single mother without her son, a hot lifeguard, and two old people. "Collecting the scraps," according to Grandpa.

I focused on Todd more than anyone else. His movements were precise, and he chewed with a purpose. He only spoke when someone else spoke to him first.

"You glad to have a break from classes for the summer, Todd?" Grandpa asked.

"Yes, sir," Todd said. "I need a break. A lot of my high school class just finished their degrees, so it'll be a little strange going back next semester with them gone. I mean, I've got other friends, but it's not the same. I'm still thinking I might reenlist." He stopped talking and went back to eating with a sigh.

"Well," Grandpa said. "I'm sure your friends care less that you're a year behind them than they do that you're back here alive. Some of my friends weren't so lucky in World War II."

I realized Todd must have been a soldier in the Gulf War. I'd learned all about it in school and remembered seeing some of the television footage I still didn't understand.

Todd nodded. "I hear you, sir."

Grandma turned to Sylvia. "How's Dane liking his new place?"

"He loves being away from home, I think," she said. "But I sure do miss him. He's been my partner-in-crime for eighteen years—half my life—so these past couple of days have been strange being in my empty house."

16

"I would imagine it hurts more when an only child moves on," Grandma said. "At least we got to practice with Ches junior moving away before Susan did. Now that was hard when our girl moved out to get married. She was only nineteen—so full of life. I'm glad you and Dane stayed nearby."

I had forgotten my mother married so young. She seemed so old now with the streaks of grey in her hair and the dark circles under her eyes that makeup didn't help hide anymore. I couldn't imagine her ever being young and fun, especially when she bitched about my clothes, telling me that flannel was only for lumberjacks. I told her it was better than letting my boobs or ass hang out of my clothes like some of the girls at my school, but she didn't understand, as always. She told me to consider adding some pink to my wardrobe, though I knew she hadn't meant with my hair color.

"What grade will you be in next year, Kincaid?" Todd asked.

Oh, my God, he was talking to me. "I'll be a junior."

"Joseph too!" Veronica laughed. "I just finished my GED."

"I always loved school," Todd said. "I envy you and Joe, still being in high school. Things were so much easier when I was a kid."

"Kid" sounded so much younger when Todd said it. Joseph looked at me and raised his eyebrows.

Grandpa coughed and took a drink of water. "Veronica, did you get the leak fixed in your roof? You don't wanna let something like that go for too long."

"Yes, Mr. Kincaid," she said. "The roofer you recommended let Joe help out and cut us a break on the labor. I had enough in savings to cover the deductible."

"You let me know if you need an advance on your salaries," Grandpa continued, looking at Joseph now. "I don't mind at all, now."

"That's not necessary, Mr. Kincaid," Joseph said. "I've still got most of my salary in savings after paying electricity. We're fine now that we got the house all paid off."

"We're here if you need us," Grandma said to Joseph. "Don't forget that."

Savings? Why would Veronica have to pay for a roof? And Joseph was saving most of his salary after electricity? They were too young to be out on their own. Their family was probably poor and needed both kids to work.

Everyone was quiet as they finished eating. Grandma got up and pulled a birthday cake out of the refrigerator and started singing to me as she sat it in the middle of the table. They all stared at me. I could have died.

"You didn't say it was your birthday," Joseph said, grinning at me.

"Because it's not. Grandma, what is this? It's not my birthday." I cringed as she slapped a paper hat on my head and snapped its elastic band under my chin. Joseph stifled a laugh. *Shit,* I thought. *She's lost her mind.*

"I know," Grandma said, lighting the number-shaped candles that spelled out sixteen. "I know it was in April, but June's not too late to celebrate since we didn't get to see you on your birthday."

My birthday was in August, not April. She was thinking of another birthday. Patrick, my brother, would have been eighteen on April 4. It felt like the ceiling might cave in on me, and I couldn't decide if I wanted to cry or throw up.

"Aww, that's so sweet," Sylvia said, turning to me. Using only my eyes, I begged her to save me. "But, Mom, our Kaykay turns sixteen on August 2, doesn't she?"

Grandma covered her mouth with her hand, still holding the matchbook. "Well, hell," she muttered. "I'm gettin' senile. It's Sarah's birthday that's in April."

Wrong again, Grandma, try October. My cousin, Sarah, was born on Halloween, a holiday she adored.

Everything would be different if Patrick were still alive. Sometimes, in the early mornings right before I would fully wake up, I'd have a fuzzy recollection of the hospital bed that had been set up in our living room, its rails shiny and silver, sparkling in the sunlight from the window. The memory always floated away before I could relish every detail. Leukemia took him at seven years old. I was only four then, almost five. Butter, my name for him since I couldn't pronounce "brother," was just gone one day, his memory fading away despite the shrine to him in our living room. I was pretty sure Dad wished I'd died instead of Patrick.

Grandma's eyes met mine, and I knew instantly she'd already realized her mistake. She dropped the matches on the countertop and sat down hard in her seat. "I'm so sorry, Kincaid," she said. "So sorry. Your brother's been on my mind lately."

19

"We'll just celebrate Kincaid's birthday early!" Grandpa announced. "It's how Patrick would have wanted it. He loved cake."

"Yeah, sure," I muttered.

Todd smiled at me and then whispered something into Veronica's ear that made her smile. I hated her at that moment, wishing Todd could whisper in my ear instead. No one spoke as they stared at me, waiting for me to do something or say something. What the hell was I supposed to do? Watching the candles flicker, I felt my life melting before my eyes.

"Go ahead, Kaykay," Sylvia said. "You have to make a wish."

I took a deep breath and glanced at Todd before I blew out the candles.

I wish for a real kiss by the end of the summer—a kiss so good it takes my mind off of everything else.

Chapter 4

I managed to get through cake and ice cream without further embarrassment after I'd yanked the stupid hat off my head. Grandma felt bad about her mistake because she wouldn't even look at me, but she'd made it worse trying to cover it up. I was relieved when Todd left—the beginning of the end of the evening. As the rest of us helped my grandparents clear the table, the kitchen suddenly felt smaller, and I couldn't get enough air. I had to get away from everyone.

"What's wrong with you, girl?" Grandpa called after me.

"I just need some air! I'm fine!" I ran to the playground and sat on one of the swings. Being outside helped, but I still wanted to cry. Thinking about Patrick always made me feel that way since I had failed him from the moment I was born.

The fireflies were just coming out. Grandpa called them "lightning bugs" when we'd catch them when I was little. I caught one and cupped my hands around it, peering in as it lit up. They were magical, flying around with their little butts lighting up an otherwise unremarkable night.

Joseph walked up beside me. "Whatcha doing?" he asked.

"Not much." I released the firefly and watched it fly away.

He sat down on the swing beside me. "Ah, catching lightning bugs."

I nodded.

"You okay?"

"Fine."

"You seemed upset about what happened with your grandma."

"It's not a big deal. I just got a little nervous with everyone looking at me."

"That's funny you'd say that—that you don't want people looking at you." He pointed at my hair. "This doesn't make you blend in too well."

"I know." *Geez, he was obsessed with my hair.*

"Are you really okay, Kincaid?"

I turned my swing toward him. "Is anyone, really?"

"Your grandpa told me about losing his oldest grandson," Joseph continued. "I didn't know until today he was your brother; I'd just assumed he was Sarah's older brother. I'm so sorry."

I turned away as a tear slipped down my cheek. He already knew more about my life than I knew about his. "Did Grandpa tell you everything about me?"

Joseph grinned. "Some, but we can probably still be friends." He stood up and rested his hand on my shoulder. "I just wanted to make sure you were okay."

I watched him walk away and turned back to the fireflies, catching another one. As I released it, I realized Joseph was still standing at the gate watching me.

"I'm sorry I was rude to you earlier—calling you princess," he said. "I hope you can forgive me. I'm a good listener if you ever want to talk."

"Thanks."

"I think we have a lot more in common than you realize."

"Maybe so." Besides being close in age, I couldn't imagine what we might have in common.

22

"I'll be here bright and early tomorrow to get started on our first project together. Wear old clothes since we'll be painting all morning."

"Okay. Goodnight."

It was still warm and sticky outside despite the growing darkness. Desperate for any breeze, I began pumping my legs until I was swinging at a nice pace to make my hair trail behind me and then blow in my face. I couldn't remember the last time I'd swung. Probably not since elementary school when I'd last had recess. I made a mental note to swing more often because it was carefree and nostalgic in exactly the way I needed that night.

Grandpa found me after everyone else had left for the night. He joined me on the swings. "I may be too old for this," he said.

"You're never too old for swings, Grandpa."

"Grandma feels really bad about what happened in there."

"I know."

We sat and listened to the crickets and tree frogs for a few minutes. I was just about to suggest we go inside when Grandpa spoke again. "We all lost Patrick, and I know it still hurts to talk about him. I miss him every day."

"You don't seem to have trouble talking to Joseph. He knew about all about Patrick, except for the fact that he was my brother. Do you tell everyone?"

Grandpa sighed and looked at his hands. "I talked to Joe because he didn't have anyone else to talk to. Sharing my thoughts on the loss of my grandson helped him."

"What do you mean? Helped him with what?"

23

"Joe didn't tell you?"

"Tell me what? What are you talking about?"

Grandpa rested his forehead on his hand and then smoothed his hair back. "His parents, child. Both of 'em. Terrible car accident about six months ago. I knew 'em from church. Joe was here helping me with a project that night. Veronica was with 'em. Got banged up pretty bad. Sylvia helped 'em get everything worked out with the life insurance and their house and stuff. I helped Joe get his license early since Veronica refused to drive after that. We invite the kids to dinner a couple of times a week. Veronica has a wild streak in her, but Joe's a good boy on the straight and narrow."

"Oh, God!" *What a jerk I was. No wonder he'd been upset when I made a comment about his parents.* "He didn't say anything."

"He might talk to you if you'd shut your yap long enough to listen."

Noted. "I'm sorry, Grandpa."

"It's not me you should be apologizing to. Best be getting inside. The mosquitoes here are as big as hummingbirds, and you don't want 'em ganging up on you."

I strolled back to my room with Grandpa, the fireflies seeming to follow us. There was a slight breeze, but the air was still too warm for it to be comforting. We were in for a hot summer; I could tell already.

"Susan tells me you've been writing poetry and also been keeping one of them diaries."

Mom told them everything. They knew all about Derek and our trouble, my writing, and Mom had probably alerted them when I'd gotten my first period and developed a need for a bra. Nothing was private.

"Or is it just a girl thing I'm not supposed to know?" continued Grandpa. "Darla sometimes turns on that microphone on the phone so we can both hear Susan."

"I prefer to call it a journal, but yeah, I write a lot. I think I want to be a writer." It was more than a want, really; it was my deepest desire—so deep I could feel it leaking from my pores all the time like a dripping faucet, the water wasted if I failed to catch it in time. "Maybe I can be when I'm older."

"That's your first mistake, Kincaid, thinking you gotta wait till you're older. Start now. I put a new notebook and pens in the nightstand drawer. I challenge you to write down every lesson you learn this summer." He looked at me with sincerity, completely opposite of my father, who'd asked about a back-up plan for my chosen life's work. "Check out the bottom drawer over there too."

I went to the drawer Grandpa had pointed at and pulled it open. Sitting there was a small, faded black box that I knew held something special to him. His portable Underwood typewriter he'd used when he'd worked for a newspaper many years ago. I lifted the box— surprisingly heavy for its size—and inhaled the musty scent of old things.

I tried not to covet material possessions, but I'd wanted his typewriter since the moment my little fingers had touched the keys at age six, right after I'd learned to read. I ran my fingers over the keys again to sense all the words already typed and yet to be typed on the tiny machine. The keys, once white, were yellowed with age from the years of use since the 1920s when it was manufactured—a gift to Grandpa from the newspaper's owner.

"I know it's an old thing," he said. "It's typed many articles on the go and probably some important letters before it came into my possession. I'd like you to have it now."

"Thanks, Grandpa." I got up to hug him. "I loved it when you let me play with this when I was little."

"You're welcome. I also suggest you get to know Joe. He's a good boy, unlike that Derek scoundrel your mom told me about."

"I really don't want to talk about Derek, Grandpa."

"Fine enough," he said, walking to the connecting door. "Don't stay up too late. I think Joe wants to get an early start painting the fence."

After Grandpa had left, I pulled the black and white stenographer's notebook out of the drawer and held it against my chest. I opened the notebook and wrote my first snippet.

Lesson 1: *Shut up long enough to listen.*

I could get to know Joe. He had introduced himself as Joseph, so I would continue to call him that until he told me otherwise. He was nothing like Derek, I could tell already, but that didn't mean we were destined to be friends.

After making sure the outside door was locked, I changed into my pajamas and sprawled out on the bed.

Using the calling card Grandma had given me, I dialed my best friend, Courtney. She picked up immediately.

"Please tell me that's you, Kincaid!"

"Yeah, it's me," I answered. "I miss you already."

"Oh, my God, me too! How long was the drive?"

"It took forever, like, six hours. My parents didn't talk to me or to each other at all the whole way here. I think they're still pissed. Thank God, I brought music with me to drown out the silence."

"I plan to do the same thing when my dad and stepmom take me and Mauve on our road trip around the Fourth. I'm still trying to talk them into staying at the motel. Wouldn't that be awesome? It's outside Hot Springs, right?"

"Yeah. A long way from Oklahoma City. Please, please keep bugging them until they give in. Wait until you see the lifeguard, Todd. He looks like all those hot guys on *90210* when they all hung out at the beach. He can rescue me anytime. He's so fine."

"Geez, Kincaid," Courtney said. "I can feel your drool starting to drip through the phone on my end. Get a grip. I guess you're over Derek?"

"I have to be. I don't think he'll ever talk to me again."

Courtney exhaled. "I have to tell you something about him."

"What?"

"Are you sure you want to know?"

"Yes. Tell me! Spill it!"

"I saw him at the video store. He was draped all over Michelle."

I was shocked. No, more than shocked, I was flabbergasted, astonished, dumbfounded. No, I was discontented, aggrieved, downright pissed. There were too many words to describe how I felt. "Michelle! She's made out with most of the tenth-grade boys. Even the ones who are gross. Why would he want her?"

"That's exactly why he wants her—she's not picky. I thought you were over him."

It was too late; I was already crying. I didn't really want to be with him after what he'd done, but I still didn't want him to be with someone else so soon, especially someone like Michelle.

"He's a prick, Kincaid. Don't cry over him. He's not worth it."

"I know, but I thought he liked me."

Lesson 2: Derek didn't really like me.

"Find you a different guy to hang out with this summer—someone better suited for you."

"What do you mean?"

"Todd," she said with a chuckle. "Do you know how old he is? Seventeen wouldn't be too old."

"No. He'll be a senior."

"That might be pushing it a bit if he's already eighteen, but not unheard of."

"In college."

"Eww! To be a senior in college, he'd have to be as old as my brother. Dude's way too old for you."

"Who cares about the ages? In five years, it won't matter."

"Are you out of your mind?" she shrieked. "He could go to jail! He's got to be at least twenty-one. Or even older."

"Calm down! I didn't say I was going to sleep with him!" While I wasn't sure I would save myself for marriage, I knew I wasn't ready for anything that serious yet. Courtney knew that, and she'd claimed to feel the same way.

"Girl, I'll get there as soon as I can to talk some sense into you. And to help you find a boy your own age."

I picked up the remote and turned on MTV. "Well, the only boy my age around here is Joseph. I have to work with him doing manual labor the whole time I'm here."

"Oh, *Joseph*, so formal. What's he like? Is he cute?"

"He thinks he is."

She giggled. "But is he?"

"I haven't thought about it. I thought he was a jerk at first, but then I found out his parents died earlier this year. It's just him and his sister now. She's pretty cool. Kinda punk-rock." I glanced at the time on the clock radio. It was almost ten o'clock. "Girl, I gotta go. I have to get up at the butt-crack of dawn to paint the fence with Joseph."

"Try to figure out if he's cute or not while you're at it, and report back tomorrow night. I'll call you."

"Sure. Goodnight."

I set the timer on the television to go off in half an hour and pulled the covers over my head to block out the light as I wondered what else Joseph was hiding.

Chapter 5

Grandpa was right about Joseph wanting to get an early start. The phone beside my bed rang right at six o'clock. I didn't even get up that early when school was in session.

"Hello?" I answered.

"Oh, good, you're up. It's Joseph."

I yawned. "I am now."

"I'll be there in ten minutes to start painting. Meet me at the playground."

"I haven't eaten yet, and I'm not dressed."

"You shouldn't paint with no clothes on. You'll get a nasty sunburn." He laughed, and I was relieved he couldn't see me blushing. "Just get there as soon as you can. It'll get hotter as the day goes on. There's hardly any shade where we'll be painting today."

"Fine." I hung up the phone and rolled out of bed, forgetting for a moment how nasty the motel carpet felt under my bare feet. I dug through my clothes and found a tank top and cut-off jean shorts to wear with some old flip-flops. I pulled my hair into a ponytail and grabbed my glasses—no time to mess with my contacts. I didn't really care what I looked like in front of Joseph for painting. I'd change later for a swim at the lake. I had a bikini I'd borrowed from Courtney that my parents didn't know about, and I planned to put it to good use even if I wasn't going to a real beach. Maybe I'd even drift out too far on a raft and let Todd rescue me.

I went to the apartment and found my grandparents in the kitchen drinking coffee with a newspaper spread out between them. There was a plate of French toast sitting in the center of the table.

"Good morning, sleepyhead," Grandma said. "We thought you were going to sleep the whole day away."

"How could I when Joseph expects me to work with him at the crack of dawn?"

"The crack of dawn was over an hour ago," Grandpa said. "Joe's smart to get an early start. The temp might go past a hundred today."

"Great," I muttered as I sat down and took two pieces of toast.

"Go easy," Grandpa said. "Eat light. Too much won't stay down if you get too hot."

"Gross, Grandpa. I'll be fine. I'm starving."

"Leave her be," Grandma said. "But you do need some sunblock, dear." She pulled a bottle out of a drawer and put it beside me. Baby's waterproof sunscreen. She wrapped her arms around my shoulder and got close to my ear. "I'm sorry about last night. I've had your brother on my mind lately, about how he would be as a grown man. I just got mixed up a little bit. I didn't mean to upset you."

"It's fine, Grandma."

She stopped talking and began washing dishes, never turning around as she scrubbed each dish at least three times. Grandpa went back to reading the paper. The toast practically melted in my mouth. I quickly ate my breakfast and headed out the door to meet Joseph. He was already setting up the paint buckets when I walked inside the playground.

"There you are," he said. "Ready to learn how to paint?" He was dressed the same as he was when I'd met him, shirtless, in old jeans and sneakers. I glanced at him several times while I applied sunscreen, wondering what it was like to have to work at fifteen to survive. Did he have other family besides Veronica? What about his grandparents? When he caught me looking, he narrowed his eyes at me and shook his head. "Shit. They told you, didn't they?"

"You could have told me."

"Yeah, that's how I greet all new people. 'Hey, I'm Joseph, my parents are dead, how are you?' The last thing I want is for people to feel sorry for me."

"I shouldn't have said what I did yesterday. It was dumb of me to say your parents forced you to work here. I'm sorry."

"Thank you."

"Do you think we can be friends?"

He bit his lip and turned away. "I don't really know you," he said, handing me a dry paintbrush. "But, I'm willing to give you a chance if you can be my friend, and not just because you feel sorry for me."

I took the paintbrush and put my hands around his for a moment. He faced me and blushed before pulling away to pour the paint.

"I'll try," I told him. "I'm sorry for what happened, but I won't pity you." He nodded. "You'll have to show me what to do."

He grinned as he put the lid back on the paint can. "Show you how to be a friend?"

"No!" I said, rolling my eyes. "Show me how to paint."

"It's not that complicated." He took my hand and helped me dip the brush in the paint. It looked like liquid chocolate flowing from the brush. "You have to wipe the excess paint off one side like this…" He scraped the brush against the side of the tray. "It keeps it from dripping on you."

"Then what? Like this?" I took the widest part of the brush and raked it sideways across the center of two posts. The paint ran down the posts making little strands between them and pooled on the ground.

"Almost. Let me show you." He took my hand again and turned the brush the other way. He outlined one post, starting from the top, using up and down strokes to stop the paint from running. Once the outline was finished, he turned the brush wide again and filled in the center using the same pattern of strokes. It was covered perfectly, and no paint dripped on the ground. "When you go horizontal, it rakes the paint off the brush when you hit the next board. Keep it vertical with the wood grain so it soaks in better, and only do one post at a time so you don't get paint stuck in between the boards. Got it?"

Lesson 3: Paint vertically to properly cover a fence post.

I nodded and demonstrated what he had shown me. "Like this?" My post wasn't quite as dark as the one we had done together, but it was close.

He tilted his head to the side and examined the post before turning to me. "See, what'd I tell you? You're a natural. Good job. You work on this section, and I'll start about ten posts down. We'll meet in the middle. You'll have to paint the tops, too, but don't use a lot of paint or it will drip down the other side and make lumps when we start to paint over there. Just light taps to get good coverage."

Joseph showed me with my brush again, this time standing closer to me with his other hand under my elbow to lift me onto my tiptoes so I could see the tops. He smelled clean, the slight woodsy scent stinging my nose. I tried to turn away but sneezed on him, almost knocking my glasses off the end of my nose. It was utterly humiliating.

"Bless you," he said, unbothered by the snot spray on his arm.

"I'm sorry," I said, reaching for my glasses. He stopped my hand and pushed my glasses back up with his hand instead. A quick glance at my paint-covered fingertips told me he had just saved me from ruining my glasses. I thought about Courtney's request to know Joseph's cuteness-level and had to break our awkward gaze. His eyes were the same warm brown as the paint, but with little flecks of green in them, like the tree leaves that surrounded us.

We worked for a couple of hours, covering one inside section of fencing before we sat down at a picnic table to take a break. By then, I was drenched in sweat, and my face stung. My breakfast was a rock sitting in my stomach. Passing out or puking—possibly both—were in my future. Joseph poured water on a clean rag and put it on the back of my neck as I leaned forward on the bench.

"I don't think we should paint anymore today," he said. "You look sick. Are you okay?"

"I don't know."

He handed me a thermos. "Need a drink?"

I shook my head and covered my face with my hands. Putting anything else in my stomach was the last thing I wanted. I took the rag off my neck and used it on my face. It felt like my skin was coming off with the rag as I wiped it.

"Go back to your room and lay down for a while. I'll go get your grandma for you."

"No, please don't get her. She'll just drive me crazy checking on me constantly."

"Are you sure?"

"Yes!" I called as I took off running toward my room.

I barely made it to my bathroom before I threw up.

Lesson 4: Don't eat too much before working in the heat.

I cleaned myself up and looked in the mirror. My face was bright red from the sun. There was a soft knock on my door followed by it creaking open.

"Kincaid?" Sylvia called. "Are you all right?"

"I'm fine," I said, walking out of the bathroom.

"Joe said he thought you were sick. You do look a little peaked. And maybe sunburnt."

"I know." I sat down on the bed. "I just got too hot. I'll be fine after I rest."

"I was hoping you'd have lunch with me today so we could talk."

I could feel myself turning green at the mere thought of lunch. "I don't feel like eating. Can we do it another day instead?"

"Sure. Lay down and rest. I've got to get back to cleaning. I left some supplies under the sink for you because Grandma said you'd be cleaning your own room while you're here. I'll still vacuum and mop once a week."

"Thanks," I said as she left the room. I stretched out on the bed under the ceiling fan and waited for my stomach to stop churning. When it finally settled down about an hour later, I got up and put some aloe vera gel on my face to take the sting out.

Lesson 5: Reapply sunscreen often when you're sweating.

Chapter 6

After a few days, I had recovered from the sunburn, and my face was peeling. I'd also learned to eat light breakfasts before working out in the heat. I wore a baseball cap I'd borrowed from Joseph while I finished painting the inside of the fence to avoid getting burnt again. The cap also helped hide my hair, which was returning to its original light brown faster than I'd hoped. The hair dye was supposed to have lasted six weeks, but I had barely gotten three out of it.

On the phone each night, Courtney wanted complete recaps of my conversations with Joseph. She always liked to analyze what guys said and how they acted. She hurt my ears with her squealing when I finally decided I was wrong about my initial assessment that Joseph wasn't cute. He wasn't drop dead in your tracks hot like Todd, but he was attractive in his own sweet way—like a lost puppy with his big brown eyes and messy hair.

Plus, Joseph was different than the boys I knew at school. More mature. He never did anything stupid like yank out my ponytail holder or snap my bra strap. He didn't burp or fart in front of me either to gross me out— a refreshing change. And he was surprisingly easy to talk to, although we'd only talked about music or movies while we painted. He liked some of the same music I liked, Nirvana and Korn, and even had appreciation for Sheryl Crow, whom I adored.

I wanted to talk to Joseph about his parents and my brother, but it didn't feel like the right time while slinging paint. I felt like a pro-painter by the time the weekend hit. We were finished by noon on Friday, so I said goodbye to Joseph right after lunch and went back to my room to change into my bikini.

It had been a couple of days since I'd seen Todd in passing. He had Wednesdays and Thursdays off, according to my grandparents. I figured he'd be lifeguarding all through the week, but there was a college-age woman with curly hair there when Todd wasn't. She didn't really talk to anyone. I was looking forward to seeing Todd back in the lifeguard stand.

Todd was standing near the water watching some little kids running around with their parents. He smiled and waved at me before returning to his post. I spread out my towel to the side of the stand, still within Todd's line of sight, and stretched out on my back.

Please, God, let him notice me again and come talk to me.

I closed my eyes to block out the bright sunlight that still bothered me through my sunglasses. I waited what felt like forever before a shadow above me blocked out the light. By then, the lake was quiet. I opened my eyes to find Todd standing above me, scanning my body. I gasped.

"Hey," he said. "You've got on sunscreen, right? The UV index is high today."

"The what?" I sat up and looked at him towering over me.

"UV index. Ultraviolet light? Don't they teach you this stuff in school? It means today has perfect conditions to get a nasty sunburn if you're not wearing adequate sunscreen."

"Grandma gave me SPF 30, so I'm good."

Todd sat down beside me on the sand, his arm brushing against mine. I could have fainted right then, but I managed to keep it together. "Still, though," he said. "Don't stay out here more than an hour before you reapply. It looks like you're already recovering from a nasty burn."

It was so sweet the way he cared about me. "Okay," I told him. "I'll be careful."

"You and Joe have made a lot of progress on the fence."

"Joseph did most of it."

"I saw you two working together." Todd laughed. "I think you helped quite a bit. At least that's what he said. Why don't you call him Joe like the rest of us?"

Everyone else did call him Joe, including his sister. "I guess because he introduced himself to me that way, and I think it suits him better than Joe."

Todd gave me a full, toothy smile, and I almost melted right there on the spot. "Well," he said. "I think Kincaid suits you better than Kaykay."

Blood rushed to my cheeks. "Yeah, Aunt Sylvia is the only person who still uses that old nickname. She's called me that since I was little."

"Sylvia's great. I used to be a mentor to her son, Dane, when he was in the scouts before I enlisted. He's a good kid."

"What's it like being in the military?"

He looked out at the families and waved at them as they left the lake, and we were alone. "You don't want to know about all that."

"Sure, I do."

Todd's smile disappeared, and he wrinkled his brow. "It's great and scary as hell all at the same time. Those men and women became my brothers and sisters. Not all of them got to come home like I did. This one guy who didn't make it home had a baby girl he never even got to meet. He carried this little photo of her in his pocket and laughed about how his kid had more hair than he did."

"What happened to him?"

"I don't want to give you nightmares."

"You won't."

"His helicopter got shot down during an airstrike in Kuwait. Twenty-three years old—the same age I am now—and his life was over just like that. Everyone on board. I was in a helicopter right behind them that didn't get hit. I'm nothing special, but I got out alive without any serious injuries. Just sheer luck, I guess. I can't explain it." He stood up and stretched. "I need to get in the water. You swim?"

I looked up at his amazing abs and wanted so badly to go in the water with him if it weren't for the tiny detail that I couldn't swim. I shook my head.

"Oh, come on," he said. "You can't swim, or you don't like to?"

I sighed. "My dad tried to teach me a couple of times, but I just sank like a rock."

Todd grabbed my hands to help me stand up. "Well, I'll just have to fix that. Come on, Kincaid, you're learning to swim this summer."

I would have protested if anyone else had asked me, but the idea of Todd teaching me to swim sounded like a dream come true. I followed him into the water until it was waist-deep on me. "You have to promise not to let me drown," I told him.

"I have a moral problem with letting others drown," he said. "Plus, I'd like to keep my job, and I'm fairly

40

certain killing the owners' granddaughter would get me fired."

"Ha!"

"Don't worry. I've taught hundreds of kids how to swim and haven't lost one yet."

"Kids?" I wasn't really a kid.

"Teenagers and adults too. I taught swimming lessons at the community pool when I was a teenager. Red Cross certified and everything."

He taught me how to float first on my back. The first couple of times, I sank immediately, and he lifted me back to the surface with his arms under my neck and knees. He kept telling me to relax and feel the water, but it was so difficult to concentrate on anything but his hand on the back of my neck. Finally, I closed my eyes and listened to his water-muffled voice telling me to imagine I was lighter than the water. It seemed to work because I felt myself floating after several tries.

"Don't freak out," Todd said. "But you're floating all by yourself. My hands are gone."

Of course, I immediately freaked out and sank, forcing me to stand up. Todd chuckled. "It's not funny!"

"It's fine," he said. "It happens to everyone when they're learning. Let's work on floating on your stomach, and then I'll stop torturing you for the day."

He put out his arms to hold me up and tried several times to get me to float on my own, but I couldn't because I was so humiliated. "I told you, I can't do this."

"You're doing fine." He put his arm around my shoulder and laughed. "I'll help you a little bit each day until you get the hang of it. It takes some kids weeks to learn."

"Hey, Todd!" Veronica called from the bank. Todd instantly pulled his arm off my shoulder and started walking toward her. I followed him like a lost puppy.

"Hey," he said to her. She handed him a towel while I picked up mine off the ground and wrapped it around myself. "You off work?"

"Yeah," she said, turning to me. "Hey, Kincaid. How are you?"

"Fine," I mumbled.

"Swimming together?" she asked.

"Teaching the kid to swim," Todd said, rubbing my head with his knuckles.

There was that word again. *Kid.*

"I've got to go," I said, practically running away from them.

"Is that really appropriate?" Veronica asked Todd while I was still within earshot.

"Stop acting jealous," he said. "She's just a kid."

"I'm not jealous, and she doesn't look like a kid, Todd," Veronica said. "I remember being her age. Be careful is all I'm saying. Don't give her the wrong idea."

Tears filled my eyes, and my heart throbbed with disappointment. He really did think of me as a kid. I walked faster and looked back at Todd and Veronica just in time to see them kissing.

Lesson 6: I am still just a kid.

Chapter 7

J oseph was standing outside my door about to knock when I walked up. "Hey," he said. "Your grandma is sending me into town for a few things. She said you might want to go."

"I don't want to get in your way. Don't you usually go by yourself?" I adjusted my towel to keep it from falling, exposing my bathing suit for a moment.

Joseph noticed and looked away, his face turning red. "And with my sister, sometimes."

"Well, she's busy sticking her tongue down Todd's throat right now, so it may just be you today. Todd was trying to teach me how to swim, but I guess he just thought the whole thing was a joke since he laughed at me. He thinks I'm a stupid little kid."

Joseph smiled and chuckled. "Okay."

I glared at him. "You think I'm a joke too! Great. I thought you'd changed your mind about me." I slammed the door in his face to keep from crying in front of him and kicked my shoes across the room.

"Kincaid!" he called from outside. "I'm sorry! I don't think you're a joke! Please, just open the door and talk to me."

I wiped the tears off my cheeks and opened the door. Joseph took a step toward me and grabbed my hands. His touch felt more electric than it had when he helped me with painting, and he dropped my hands quickly. I looked him in the eyes and crossed my arms, waiting for him to say something.

"You're not a joke," he said. "I didn't mean to hurt your feelings. And Todd can be a real dick sometimes. I'll help you learn how to swim, and I promise I won't laugh at you."

I had to look at the floor because I couldn't handle looking at Joseph any longer. Tears welled up in my eyes again and dripped on my bare feet. The strangest thing in the world happened next. Joseph stepped forward and wrapped his arms around me. I'd only ever cried on my parents' shoulders before. I didn't even know what the hell I was crying about anymore, and I couldn't stop. But afterward, it felt like I had known Joseph far longer than a week.

Lesson 7: *Unexpected hugs are the best ones.*

"It's all right," he said as I pulled away. "I think you need more than a trip to the hardware store. Come hang out with me and my friends tonight."

"Are you sure? I—"

"Wash your face and put on some clothes. Meet me in the main apartment in fifteen minutes. I need to talk to your grandparents."

"That'll barely give me enough time to put on makeup and fix my hair."

"Fine," he said, closing the door. "Make it twenty."

After the quickest shower in history, I got dressed in a pink bodysuit and shortalls. I dried my hair and pulled it back at the sides. I put on makeup with lightning speed and put in my contacts. It was the first time all week I'd even tried to make myself presentable. I wondered what Joseph had planned for us. He thought I needed more than an errand trip. What did he have in mind? I grabbed my sandals and headed for my grandparents' apartment.

Grandpa and Joseph were sitting on the couch, and Grandma walked out of the kitchen with iced tea for them. "Hey, sweetheart," she said to me. "You look pretty."

"Thanks, Grandma."

"Joe wants to take you to see a movie tonight with him and some of his friends," Grandpa said. "We told him it was all right as long as he gets you home by ten."

I looked at Joseph, who smiled at me. "That is, if you want to go with me," he said. "We're going for pizza first. It's me and four other people, all my age or a year younger."

"And we know all the kids from church," Grandma added. "Good kids. I think it'll be good for you to go out with kids who don't get into trouble." *So much for my slate being wiped clean.*

"So, do you want to go out with me?" Joseph asked.

I had to admit going to a movie with him sounded better than watching MTV alone in my room again. "Sure," I said. "It sounds like fun."

Grandpa pulled out his wallet and handed me ten dollars. "Have fun, Kincaid. Drive safe, Joe."

"Of course, sir."

I followed Joseph to his truck, a silver Chevy. "Are we picking up anyone else?"

"No, they'll meet us at the mall. We all hang out there since it's got the pizza place and the movie theater right there. Technically, I'm only supposed to drive to and from work, church, or school, but none of the officers in town will ticket me. They all knew my parents."

"Well, there's that, and Grandpa says you're a good boy on the straight and narrow path."

"Definitely straight," he said with a laugh as he started the truck. "But I don't know about a narrow path, though I do try to avoid doing anything that would get me pulled over or cause an accident."

I instantly recognized the music from the CD that started playing because it was one in my collection. The soundtrack to *My So-Called Life*—a show that's official cancellation announcement within the last month had devastated me. "Oh my gosh! I have this CD too!"

"It's actually Veronica's," he said. "But the show wasn't half-bad. I watched a couple of episodes with her."

"I loved that show. I seriously wanted to be Angela."

"Is that why you dyed your hair—to look like her?"

"Hers was red—not pink—and I dyed my hair because I felt like it. I got tired of being boring, and I thought it would piss off my parents."

"Red, pink, not a big difference there. And wouldn't getting arrested for stealing cigarettes piss them off enough?"

"The whole thing was a misunderstanding."

"So?"

"What?"

"Spill it. Tell me what happened."

"Didn't my grandparents tell you everything already?"

"I already told you all I know. I want to hear it from you."

"There was this guy…"

"Isn't there always?"

"Derek. He was a skater, new at my school, and I really liked him. He didn't seem to care much about getting to know me when I first introduced myself. But during spring break, I ran into him, and we started hanging out. He was stuck taking his little brother to the library activities, and I was there anyway helping out. He told me he wanted to hang out sometime, so we talked every day that week. We were hanging out at the end of the week, and he asked me to wait outside a convenience store downtown. I waited for him for ten minutes or so. When he came running out, he threw some packs of cigarettes in my arms, kissed me, and then took off running."

"He kissed you and threw stolen merchandise at you? Sounds like a real winner."

"One of the workers was chasing him."

"And that makes it okay? He sounds like an asshole."

The whole thing sounded more ridiculous each time I retold the story. "I was so shocked by the whole thing, I just stood there like an idiot. If I had any sense at all, I would've run while the worker chased after Derek."

Joseph shook his head as he pulled into the parking lot of the hardware store. He parked, killed the engine, and turned to me. "Had you ever been kissed before, when Derek kissed you?"

"He only kissed me on the cheek, but it didn't mean anything because he found someone else already, some girl who's made-out with half the school."

"If it wasn't on the lips, then it didn't count. No spin-the-bottle or anything else?" he asked. "We started playing spin-the-bottle around here at eleven or twelve. Not much to do in a small town, you know? But I don't usually kiss and tell."

Lesson 8: Kisses on the cheek don't count.

I shook my head, embarrassed that I was almost sixteen, and my lips had never touched someone else's. "Guys don't think of me like that. At my school, they all think I'm kind of nerdy and weird for wanting to be a writer. Derek went to parties and stuff, but I never got invited."

Joseph pushed my hair out of my face. "Derek's a jerk, and trust me, there are guys who think of you like that." He got out of the truck, walked over to my side, and spoke through the window, which was opened just a bit. "I'll be right back, unless you want to come inside with me?"

"I'll wait here."

I wasn't sure guys really thought of me like that. *Was he talking about himself or guys in general?*

Dylan and Brenda on *90210* had gone to a movie for their first date. *Was this a date?*

Chapter 8

After the hardware store, Joseph drove us to the mall. It was a longer distance than I anticipated with all the tourist traffic. He changed out the CD to Nirvana's *MTV Unplugged* for the drive. I looked out the window and let the raw emotion of Kurt Cobain's voice drift through my heart. He would never get any older. Never make any more music. He was gone—dead like Joseph's parents. Dead like my brother.

"You usually talk more," Joseph said. "What's up? Are you still upset about something?"

"I'm fine. I'm just enjoying the music. Don't worry, I won't cry on you again."

"It's no big deal. Girls cry a lot more than guys do from what I've noticed with my sister and my girlfriends."

"Girlfriends?" I teased. "How many girlfriends are we talking about here?

"Well, friends who are girls."

"Who all will be there tonight?"

"Dustin, Amy, Heather, and Kevin if he doesn't have to babysit his little brother."

"What are they like?"

"We've all known each other since kindergarten—all but Heather. She moved here a couple of years ago and is a grade below us. I think they'll like you."

"Do they know I'm coming?"

"No, but I promise they won't think you're weird or nerdy. They're all really nice. And who knows, maybe me and my friends are the weird, nerdy ones at our school?" He grinned at me.

Joseph's friend, Dustin, was a teddy bear of a guy trying too hard to look older with a mustache barely visible on his upper lip. His bleached hair stuck out in corkscrew curls all over his head, and he played tuba in the high school band according to the "tuba-line" t-shirt he wore. Amy was the friendliest and greeted me with a compliment to my outfit. She was pretty and perky, with dark wavy hair that reached her shoulders. She wore a flowery dress and a gold necklace with a tiny musical note charm. Dustin put his arm around her when she sat down, and I figured out they were a couple.

Heather was a blond about my height. She had serious eyes and a friendly smile but seemed more reserved than the others with her hair pulled back in a bun so tight it stretched her face at the temples. She greeted Joseph with a hug. "How are you doing?" she asked. I wanted to dump her milkshake all over her perfect bun and immediately felt ridiculous for my jealousy. Heather sat down beside Amy.

"Good," Joseph said. "Working hard at the motel. I'm turning Kincaid into a professional painter."

"Don't forget about the summer reading list," Heather said.

"How could I when you call twice a week to remind me?" Joseph asked her. He turned to me. "Heather's in AP English, so she's helping me catch up with some of the work I missed last semester."

Heather turned to me with a warm smile that instantly relaxed her face. "Joe told me you want to be a writer. What do you write?"

He had talked to her about me? "Poetry, mainly, but I'd love to write a novel someday," I said.

"That's so cool," she said, stretching her legs in front of her with her toes pointed at the floor. "I love to read and draw. Sometimes, I draw out scenes I've read in books. I think it would be awesome to illustrate children's books for a living." With her graceful and effortless movements, I would have guessed she wanted to be a ballet dancer.

"You should see the one she drew from *Alice's Adventures in Wonderland*," a male voice said from behind me. A tall boy with long jet-black hair joined us and practically fell into the chair beside Heather. He wore dark eyeliner, multiple earrings in both ears, and black nail polish. I was shocked when he kissed Heather full on the lips in front of us. "Hey, babe."

"Kevin," she said to the boy. "This is Joe's friend, Kincaid. Her grandparents run the motel where he works, Mr. and Mrs. Kincaid from church. Kincaid, this is my boyfriend, Kevin." Maybe I didn't hate her.

Kevin extended his hand to shake mine—the only one of them to do so. "It's good to meet you, Kincaid."

They were all kind to me, but Kevin was the most genuinely polite with me and everyone else, despite the disparaging looks the wait-staff gave him when they took our order at the pizza parlor.

Lesson 9: Looks really can be deceiving.

A group of four high school guys in tank tops and board shorts came into the pizza parlor while we were waiting for our food. They stood beside our table. "Oh, look, it's the virgin brigade," one guy said. They all laughed together. There were guys like them at my school, too—the kind who seemed to share a brain between them.

Kevin stood up and got in the main guy's face, taller than him by a couple of inches. The guy took a step back as Kevin smiled. "But, yet, here we are with dates, and it looks like it's just you and your sausage brigade. Move along now. Go be dicks over there."

"Fine, tiny dancer boy, we're leaving," the guy said. "Don't get your pantyhose in a twist."

Joseph's friends laughed as the mean guys walked away. Kevin had pointed out a fact the jerks couldn't argue with. I turned to them. "What's that all about?" I asked. "Are they all just jerks?"

"Those assholes think we're lame and give us crap all the time," Joseph said. "'Tiny dancer boy' is Kev's basketball nickname."

"I don't think you're lame," I said to Joseph, then I looked toward the table of mean guys, who'd started making kissing faces at us. I rolled my eyes and turned to Kevin. "Tiny dancer boy? Explain, please."

Kevin laughed and reached for Heather's hand. "Heather and I met at the dance studio downtown. She's a ballet dancer, and I've done ballet, tap, and jazz since I was a kid. I'm one of only four male dancers in the studio. Most of the guys on the basketball team don't care that I dance, but some guys make fun of me. I don't really care what they think. At least when I take an elbow during the game, I have the balance to not fall on my ass like they do."

"You do ballet?" I asked Kevin. I knew some guys did… but in Arkansas? There was definitely more to him than I initially thought.

"Oh yeah," Joseph said. "He's been dancing since he was little. He's really good."

Kevin shrugged his shoulders.

"He's better than me at ballet," Heather added.

We all laughed and talked while we enjoyed our pizza. Heather and Kevin ate more than the rest of us. Must have been all the calories they'd burned dancing. I had never seen such a tiny girl eat almost a whole pizza by herself in one sitting.

Heather and Amy dragged me to the restroom with them before the movie. As soon as they confirmed we were alone, they both squealed, and each grabbed one of my hands. I stared at them, bewilderment settling over me. "What?"

"Joe never brings a girl with him," Amy said. "I'm just so happy he finally did."

"It's usually just the five of you?"

"Yeah," Heather said. "I guess you know what happened to his parents?"

I nodded and looked in the mirror to check my hair. "My grandparents have been helping him out with a job. I'm staying there for the summer."

"When it happened, Joe missed school for two months," Amy said. "He came back, but he wasn't really himself until about a month ago. I've known him since kindergarten. He's a really sweet guy."

"He seems like it. My grandparents seem to love him."

"Your grandparents are so cool," Amy said. "We know them from church. They always chaperone the teenager events. Why haven't you come with them to church before?"

"My family lives in Oklahoma City. It's a six-hour drive."

"Oh," Amy said. "We didn't realize."

"Do you like Joe?" Heather asked me.

"Of course, I do. I think we're going to be good friends."

"No," she said. "Do you *like him* like him?"

Blood rushed to my cheeks. "I don't know yet. Maybe?"

Heather smiled at Amy. "Okay, I have to tell you something, and you can't say anything to him," she said to me. "Promise me?"

"Okay."

"I talked to Joe on the phone last night," Heather said. "That's when he told me about meeting you and working with you all week…"

"Oh, just tell her already!" Amy interrupted.

Heather giggled. "Kincaid, Joe likes you."

"As in *likes you* likes you," Amy said.

As if I wasn't already nervous enough meeting Joseph's friends, with the new knowledge that he liked me, I worried I might be sick as well. I tried to settle my nerves as we all walked across the mall parking lot to the detached movie theater. We all agreed to see a movie called *Congo*. Joseph had already bought my ticket by the time I pulled the money from Grandpa out of my purse.

"You can pay next time," he said.

Next time? He planned on a next time?

We sat at the back of the theater as the previews started. I was at the end of the aisle next to Joseph, and the others sat on the other side of him. My palms were drenched in sweat that I kept wiping on my shortalls. Luckily, he didn't try to hold my hand, and they dried up as I became engrossed in the movie. When a part made me jump, I grabbed Joseph's arm before I realized what I was doing.

He turned to me in the darkness, and I could see the light from the projector reflected in his eyes. "You okay?" he whispered. I nodded and let go of him. He pushed the armrest out of the way and moved closer to me. I thought I would die when he put his arm around me. He left it there for the rest of the movie.

After some good-hearted teasing with Amy about her sharing the name of the gorilla in the movie, Joseph and I left so he could get me home before ten o'clock. As we walked to his truck, a girl called out to him and came running over when he turned around. She was trying way too hard to get noticed in her tight black dress and ridiculous high heels.

"Hey," he said to the girl. She looked at me. "Kincaid, this is Mindy. She goes to my school. Kincaid's grandparents own the motel outside of town where I work."

"Hi," I said. Her eyes were like daggers stabbing me. I had seen that look before but never directed at me. No one had ever been jealous of me.

"I was hoping we'd get to hang out sometime this summer," she said, tucking her hair behind her ears.

"I've got work and schoolwork to catch up on, so I don't have much free time right now," Joseph said. "I'm sure I'll see you at school in August. It was good seeing you, Mindy. I have to get Kincaid home before her curfew. Bye."

We left her standing on the sidewalk near the mall as we drove away. I laughed, both at the absurdity of Mindy and what Heather and Amy had told me in the restroom.

Joseph glanced at me. "What?" he said, laughing with me. "Oh, Mindy?"

"She's something, isn't she? I think she likes you."

"Yeah, I know she does."

"You don't like her?" I asked.

"Not even a little bit."

"Why not?"

"She rarely talked to me before my parents died, then she started acting like she was my best friend or girlfriend or something, like she had to save me. She acts all nice to everybody, but then she talks bad about them behind their backs. Phony and two-faced."

"I know some people like that."

"I don't like to be around people like that." He turned up the volume on the CD player in his truck. "This song's my favorite." It was Nirvana's "Pennyroyal Tea," one of my favorites as well.

"Why did those guys call you and your friends the virgin brigade?" I asked when the song was over.

"They're referring to the purity pledge," Joseph said. "We all signed it at church with some other people from school."

"All your friends signed it?"

"Not all of them, but the ones you met tonight did. A lot of people don't understand why we'd want to save ourselves for marriage and think we're religious freaks, but I don't want to mess up and disappoint my parents. And it's not like we don't ever have any fun."

"Like those games of spin-the-bottle?"

Joseph laughed. "Those actually happened at church parties, believe it or not. We can still go out on dates and have relationships; they just won't involve sex."

"My parents don't go to church, but I've always been curious about it. I've thought saving myself for marriage sounded like a good plan for a while now. Sex seems to be a much bigger deal than people make it out to be. There was a girl at my school who had a baby last year—at thirteen. I guess the fear of getting pregnant or an STD has been my main reason for staying a virgin—that and my social awkwardness—since I'm not really religious." My face reddened. All I had done was open my mouth to let verbal diarrhea spill all over both of us.

He chuckled. "It's not really about religion or the church. It's more of a spiritual thing that's personal for everyone, you know? You can be a good person who never sets foot inside a church just as easily as you can be a bad person who's there every time the doors are open. You can hang out with me at church if you come with your grandparents on Sunday, but if you don't want to, I get it."

He was absolutely perfect. No pressure about anything. "I'm sure I'll see you there."

"I've told you my favorite Nirvana song," he said. "What's yours?"

"I think I like 'Something in the Way' the best, even if it's really sad."

"No, that's a great one." He skipped ahead on the CD to play it for me.

By the time the song was over, we were back at the motel with a half-hour to spare before my curfew. My grandparents were sitting outside waiting as we pulled up, pretty much spoiling any hopes I had for a goodnight kiss. "I guess they're waiting up for me. How embarrassing."

"You don't really realize how nice it is to have someone waiting up for you until you don't have it anymore," Joseph said as he got out of the truck. I was an idiot for continuing to shove my foot in my mouth around him. He walked over to my side to let me out. My grandparents waved to us and stepped back inside, turning off the outside light. The only light remaining was from the fixture outside my room as Joseph walked me to the door.

"Thank you for inviting me tonight."

"I hope you had fun," he said as I unlocked my room.

"I did. Your friends are great."

"We go to the movies or video store every weekend. Maybe you can come with me again." He took a step back, then stepped forward again and kissed me on the cheek, awakening every single nerve in my body. "Goodnight, Kincaid."

I watched him walk back to his truck and drive away, unable to move until he was out of sight.

Lesson 10: Kisses on the cheek don't count...until they do.

Chapter 9

A unt Sylvia picked me up early Saturday morning for a day of shopping. It was so much more fun shopping with her than my mother because Sylvia offered helpful comments instead of criticizing every item I tried on. I didn't really care about following every single trend; I just wanted to wear what I liked as long as it was comfortable.

I ended up buying two outfits with some of the money my parents had left me. I still had plenty for the rest of the summer. Sylvia and I ate burgers at the mall food court after we'd finished our morning shopping. I saw Amy and Heather coming out of a store with a woman who had to be Heather's mom, and they waved at me.

"Making friends already, that's good," Sylvia said.

"Maybe," I said. "They're Joseph's friends, but we all hung out here last night and went to a movie."

"Was it a date, Kaykay?"

I could feel the redness in my face deepening. "I don't know. Maybe."

"Joe's a sweet boy. Tell me about the boy who got you into trouble."

I rehashed my story for the third time since arriving for my visit. Sylvia nodded and listened, never interrupting me.

"Sounds like you've learned your lesson, haven't you?"

"I guess so. Mom and Dad expect me to be perfect. I don't think they'll ever forgive me. All they did was yell at me. Later, they barely talked to me or each other."

"And what do you think that means?"

"I don't know. I guess they're still pissed."

Sylvia sighed. "I don't think everything is as clear-cut as that, Kincaid."

"What are you talking about?"

Before Sylvia could answer, Veronica walked up beside our table. "Hey!" she said. "I was hoping to find you." Veronica took out a package of hair dye from her bag and showed it to Sylvia. "I need some help with this."

I looked at her hair more closely and noticed the lighter roots showing under her chestnut-colored hair. Her original color was light brown like mine.

"I promised Kincaid a whole day of shopping," Sylvia said. "But I could help you tonight or tomorrow."

Veronica shook her head. "I have to get this done today. I have a date tonight that's supposed to be really special, and I want to look my best. It turned out so well when you helped me last time."

I didn't like that Veronica thought of me as a little kid, but I didn't want to disappoint her because she was Joseph's sister. Sylvia turned back to me as I spoke. "I'm actually tired of shopping," I told them. "Let's go dye your hair, Veronica." I hoped we would go to her house so I could see Joseph again.

"Great!" she squealed. "Let me go tell my friends I have a ride." She ran off toward a group of girls her age who were waiting nearby.

I turned back to Sylvia. "What were you saying about Mom and Dad?"

She didn't want to reply, I could tell, but she did. "I don't think they're getting along very well with each other."

"That's impossible. They've been married for a long time. They're fine."

"But are they? Just keep an open mind, Kaykay. Divorces happen sometimes, even if people have been married a long time."

"They're fine," I said again as Veronica came back.

We went to Sylvia's house to help Veronica with her hair. They set up everything at the kitchen table. I sat watching them and quietly listened to them talk while I looked through the magazines Veronica had bought at the mall. I read *Seventeen* at home and thought Veronica might be a bit too old for it since I learned she'd just turned nineteen. After Sylvia and Veronica started talking, I figured they'd forgotten I was there. I wasn't paying much attention until I heard Veronica mention sex. That got my attention.

"I mean, I've made out with guys before," she said. "It just never lasted long enough to get to sex. I think I'm ready now. Todd's such a good guy, and I know he's the one. It'll be so romantic for my first time to be with him."

"Do you really think everyone's first time is all romantic and dreamy?" Sylvia asked her. "Girl, you have no idea. My first time wasn't romantic at all."

"Why not?" Veronica asked. I hoped they wouldn't remember I was still in the room as I continued to flip through the magazine pages.

"Because of how it happened. I was seeing this guy named Mitch. We'd been seeing each other for a few weeks and hadn't really talked about where our relationship was going. Before our date, he had already bought a condom at the drug store—that should've been a red flag. He drove us to the middle of nowhere near a field with only the moonlight to guide us. He grabbed some paper towels out of the glove box of his car and led me to a clearing behind some trees. He spread out a beach towel on the ground. It was like nothing I'd ever imagined."

"Did it hurt?"

"Yeah, it felt like I was being ripped apart from the outside in because I don't think I was truly ready. It was over pretty quickly, and I was bleeding a lot afterward. I stuffed those damn paper towels in my panties, and he drove me home."

Oh, my God. I'd never heard anything like that before. It was terrifying.

"How old were you?" Veronica asked. "Did you love him?"

"I was barely eighteen, and it was never about me not loving him. I loved that boy more than anyone else in the world. More than I loved myself. That gets dangerous when you're a teenager. The problem was, I don't think he loved me. Deep down, I probably knew that at the time, but I kept having sex with him anyway. In cars, park restrooms, secluded outdoor places…"

"Sylvia!" Veronica exclaimed as they walked to the kitchen sink to rinse her hair.

"I didn't use good judgment. Most guys don't think about sex the same way most women do. They can separate out the physical and the feelings. The lines blur for women and get worse each time the act is over with someone who doesn't love you. If I could go back and do it all over again…well, maybe I wouldn't have given it away so freely. I would have waited for someone who thought I was special. The only thing good that came out of the relationship was Dane."

"But I know Todd is my someone special," Veronica said. "He says he loves me, and I know I love him too. We'll probably get married. We've been through a lot together already."

"I'm not saying he isn't," Sylvia said. She turned to me. I guess she did remember I was there. "I hope you're taking notes, Kaykay. This could be you soon." I nodded. "Veronica, I know Todd is a good man; I've known him since he was a boy. If he is your someone special, then he won't pressure you. He'll wait until you're ready and will never make you feel bad about yourself, and he won't be abusive and make you feel like less of a person like my ex-husband."

I knew Sylvia had left Uncle Roy, but I never knew he wasn't Dane's father. The conversation was getting more interesting and more adult than I'd expected.

"You and Todd have both been through a lot, him with the war and you with the accident and loss of your parents. Even without things like that, relationships can be difficult and intense, especially at your age." Sylvia sat down across from us. "I was devastated when I met my ex-husband, Roy. He found me when I was vulnerable. I'd just found out I was pregnant, and Mitch was gone. I knew I didn't love Roy, but I had sex with him the first night we met because I just wanted someone to hold me. I was surprised when he proposed two weeks later. He said all the right things about how he'd take care of me and the baby like it was his own. And then, in the heat of the moment, I did something I knew was wrong that still hurts eighteen years later—I told him I would marry him."

"You didn't love your husband?" Veronica asked. "How can you marry someone you don't love?"

"I thought I would grow to love him since he claimed to love me so much, but instead, over time, he made me feel worthless, and I started to believe him. He always reminded me I was the whore who got pregnant at eighteen and told me no one else would want me and my bastard child. Even though Mitch turned out to be a jerk, at least he wasn't abusive like Roy."

"God, did Roy hit you?" Veronica asked. "Todd would never do that."

"No," Sylvia said with a sigh as she rested her face in her hands. "He never laid a hand on me. Sometimes I wish he had hit me, though, as stupid as it sounds. Bruises and broken bones heal much easier than wounds from words. I think it would have been easier to walk away then. Instead, I stayed with the asshole for four years because I thought he was the only person who would love me since Mitch had abandoned me without a word. It took a lot of detox to get over those things and trust another man. I haven't dated anyone else until this year. And I'm finally finishing my accounting degree in the fall. I put everything I had into raising Dane, so I only took night classes when I wasn't at work."

"So, you never saw Mitch again?" I asked, hoping she would still tell us more.

Sylvia shook her head and wiped a tear from her eye. "The last day I saw Mitch was a real emotional day for me. I gathered a little courage and told him I couldn't continue things how they were. That I was tired of being a secret he seemed ashamed of. I told him I wanted an actual relationship because I was in love with him, and if he didn't want that, I never wanted to see him again."

"Wow," Veronica said as she looked at me.

The same woman who had stayed in a loveless marriage had given an ultimatum to the man she loved. It was like something out of a movie or a torrid romance novel.

"I worked at the motel then, too, under the previous owners," Sylvia said. "I asked Mitch to meet me at the lake by the docks if he loved me and wanted a relationship with me. I waited there all night before I accepted that he wasn't coming and went home. I cried on and off for a couple of days. A week later, I suspected I was pregnant, and the next week I had it confirmed by a doctor. Home pregnancy tests weren't available around here until a few years later. It was 1976, so I didn't have any other options at the time to know for sure. I tried to contact Mitch, but his roommates said he had bailed on them and skipped out on rent, leaving his car behind and everything he owned inside—his clothing, records, and even a straight razor his grandfather had given him."

Now it was more of a mystery novel, and I was more interested than ever. "Did you try to find him again, after divorcing Uncle Roy?"

"I contacted his family once pretending to be calling from a company to say he'd won a prize. The lady on the phone yelled at me for being so insensitive to call a family who was missing their adult child and then hung up. Later, I did some more research and learned they'd reported him missing that same summer I got pregnant. He wasn't close with his family, so I always figured he'd gone to Canada and left everything behind like he'd joked about when we were hanging out. I've done more research at the college library trying to find him, but I haven't had any luck. I figure he changed his name when he moved and doesn't want to be found. I hate it for Dane."

"Dane's never mentioned to me that Roy wasn't his dad. Does he know who his father is?"

Sylvia nodded. "I've shown him the only picture I have of Mitch." She stopped what she was doing and walked over to a china cabinet along the wall. She took out a small silver frame and showed it to us. The man was devastatingly handsome, with messy blond hair and a friendly smile. He wore a necklace with a shark tooth dangling from it.

Veronica and I looked at each other as Sylvia returned the photo to its hiding place. I watched Sylvia dry and style Veronica's hair. Veronica stood up and walked to the mirror in Sylvia's hallway bath. "This looks incredible!" she said. "Todd won't be able to resist me tonight. And we'll be so much closer tomorrow. I can handle it if it hurts a bit the first time. It will get better, right?"

Sylvia shook her head at me as Veronica came back into the kitchen. She grabbed Veronica by the shoulders and reminded her to use protection. Then she told her what stuck with me more than anything else.

Lesson 11: It's not about how much it hurts the first time; it's about how much it hurts when it's over.

Chapter 10

We dropped off Veronica at Todd's house, and he was waiting in the driveway for her. She got out of the car and ran to him, jumping into his arms and kissing him.

"I don't think I got through to her at all," Sylvia said as we drove away. "Hopefully, something I said stuck with you. I just don't want her to get hurt. I wouldn't want that for you either."

I didn't know what to say.

"I'm sorry I upset you with what I said about your parents," she continued. "I know it's scary to think about them splitting up, but I wanted you to prepare yourself if this marriage retreat doesn't work."

"What are you talking about? Marriage retreat? I don't even know what the hell that is."

"Crap," she muttered. "I thought they would have told you. I shouldn't have said anything. It wasn't my place."

"You have to tell me now, or I'll ask Grandma and Grandpa about it."

"I heard Mom and Dad talking about it, and I just assumed you knew. I'm sorry, Kaykay. It's kind of a last-ditch effort for them to see if they can stay married before they decide to separate. It doesn't mean they don't love you."

Lesson 12: Parents suck when they lie.

"No, it just means they don't love each other, right? It means they can't be grown-ups and get their shit together. People don't even try anymore. Half of my friends' parents are divorced."

Sylvia sighed. "It's not that simple, Kaykay. Losing your brother changed their relationship forever. A lot of marriages can't survive that much pain."

"They seemed to get through it fine when I was little! Why now?"

"Sweetheart, I can't speak for them," she said as we pulled to a stop at the motel. She grabbed my shoulders and made me face her. "You need to sit down with both of them when they come back to get you, and they will be able to explain everything. Your mom's hurting a lot, and I'm sure your dad is too. Maybe they just need some help getting through it."

"I don't want to talk about it anymore," I said. "They're not the only ones in pain; I miss Patrick too!" I got out and slammed the car door. Joseph's truck was in the front parking lot. I looked around, wondering where he might be as I watched Sylvia drive away.

"Kincaid, come inside!" Grandpa called from his door, startling me. "I want you to meet a dear friend of ours who's passing through."

"Coming, Grandpa, just let me put my stuff away."

I dropped my bags off in my room and combed my hair. As I stared at my reflection in the mirror, I took several deep breaths to calm down. My face was blotchy and red, either from my anger or the heat. I grabbed my pressed powder and dusted over the brightest areas before I headed to the apartment.

When I walked in, Joseph was sitting on the couch with a familiar long-haired Hispanic man who looked

68

like he was in his seventies. Grandma and Grandpa were sitting in their recliners across from them.

Joseph scooted to the center cushion beside the man and motioned for me to sit down, but just I stood there, unsure of what to do. Two thoughts were running through my mind. One, Joseph was wearing a sleeveless shirt that highlighted the suntanned muscles in his arms. That alone was enough to make me blush. Two, the familiar man bore a striking resemblance to my favorite poet of all time, Eduardo Martinez, who had appeared much younger in the book jacket photos I'd seen at the library. I adored his poetry, some of the most beautiful I'd ever read.

"Ed, this is my namesake, Kincaid," Grandpa said. "She's Susan's daughter and has aspirations to be a writer like you. Kincaid, this is Eduardo Martinez. You might have read some of his stuff. He's made quite the name for himself."

My heart jumped into my throat. How was it possible that my grandfather, of all people, knew this amazing poet? "Eduardo Martinez! Oh my! I love your poetry. I think I've checked out all of your books from the school library."

He stood up and shook my hand. "Always pleased to meet a fellow word-slinger," he said. "I hear you're handy too. Joseph was telling me about your fence painting project."

"Oh," I said, finally sitting down. I could feel a slight tremble in my hands from all the excitement. "It's all Joseph. He's the handy one. I'm just trying not to mess up all his good work."

"Don't sell yourself short, Kincaid," Grandma said with a wink. "Joe's been bragging on you, saying you've been a big help. "

"I'm just telling the truth," Joseph said to her and then grinned at me.

I could feel myself blushing again. I couldn't believe I'd just met someone so famous, and now the boy I maybe liked—okay, probably liked—was bragging on me to my grandparents and the famous person in the room. It was a great distraction from thinking about my parents, and I couldn't stop a giggle from escaping my lips.

Joseph stayed to eat dinner with us at Grandma's request. She didn't want him eating alone since he'd mentioned Veronica going out of town for the night with a friend. I knew the truth. He didn't want to stick around his house thinking about his sister's imminent deflowering.

Ed Martinez was full of surprises. I'd only read his poetry; I never knew he led such an adventurous life with his wife, who had died recently. They'd spent their lives traveling the world, just the two of them. He loved her dearly, judging by how he spoke of her and what he'd written about her in his romantic poetry.

"The first trip we ever took was a road trip out to Colorado," he said. "We hadn't been married very long at the time—both of us about twenty-two or three, but we'd been in love since we were not much older than you two." He looked at Joseph and me. "We didn't have more than twenty dollars to our names, but we hitchhiked and made our way out there. Then we got odd jobs with the railroad and the mines until we had enough money saved up to travel again. Took us five years."

"What kind of mines, Mr. Martinez?" Joseph asked. "Was it coal?"

"No, son, gold. Now, Cripple Creek is a gamblin' town, chock-full of tourists. Rosa always adored that little place. We made our last trip there two years ago before she got sick with the cancer."

"We were so sorry to hear about Rosa's passing, Ed," Grandpa said. "She was a beautiful soul. I hated that we couldn't make it to her memorial. Our kids always adored her when you'd visit us."

"She adored them as well," Ed said. "Rosa always had a love for children. It's a pity the good Lord didn't see fit to bless us with any of our own."

I learned that Grandpa and Ed had known each other since they were boys out in California before Grandpa's family moved to Arkansas. They'd met up again by chance or fate during the war after Grandpa enlisted. Ed had been at Pearl Harbor the day of the attack—the attack that had convinced Grandpa to enlist in the first place. Ed's novel about the whole experience would be published in the fall, and I couldn't wait to get my hands on it.

Rosa had died only two months before Ed's visit to the motel. It was a trip they'd planned to take together, knowing it might be her last. Ed had promised Rosa on her deathbed he'd take the trip anyway to see his dearest friend again. The whole story was beautiful, tragic, and romantic—his love for her conveyed in every word he spoke, like his poetry.

71

Ed kept us up late telling stories about his adventures with his wife. I couldn't imagine living a life like his. Living like that would give me plenty to write about— more than the boring life I'd led so far. Joseph was entranced with Ed's stories as well, asking specific questions regarding each adventure.

Rosa and Ed had scuba-dived in Hawaii, climbed mountains in Colorado, bathed in the hot springs in Arkansas, kissed under the Eiffel Tower in Paris, hiked through Alaska, and walked across The Great Wall of China. I'd never thought to study the life of my favorite poet before, and now I was certain he was the most fascinating person I'd ever met.

Chapter 11

When everyone tired out, Grandpa asked Joseph to show Ed to his room. It was room twenty, farthest away from mine so he would have plenty of quiet time to write. I said goodnight to my grandparents after that and went to my room.

I had just taken out my contacts when someone knocked on my outside door. I grabbed my glasses, turned on the porch light, and looked out the peephole, grinning as I saw Joseph there.

"Hey," Joseph said as I opened the door. "Did you have fun shopping?"

"Yeah. I saw Amy and Heather at the mall, and then we ran into Veronica and helped her dye her hair at Sylvia's house this afternoon. I didn't know you were coming for dinner tonight."

"Neither did I. They wouldn't take no for an answer after I slipped and told them about my sister going out of town tonight. At least I didn't tell them who she was going with. I guess you know about that?"

"She said something to Sylvia, I think."

"I'm trying not to think about it," he said as he leaned against the wall. "I'm kind of used to being alone. Veronica doesn't like to be at the house much."

I walked outside and closed the door behind me and then sat on the bench near the outside wall. "I like being alone sometimes…"

"But sometimes it gets lonely." Joseph sat down beside me. "Do you miss your brother?"

"I don't really remember much about him. I was only four when he died."

"I didn't realize you were so young when it happened. Your grandpa just told me it was cancer when Patrick was a kid."

"Yeah, leukemia. He was seven." I looked down at my hands and spun around the silver ring on my middle finger to keep from crying. "The only reason my parents had me was to try to save him. If my blood had matched his, I could have been a bone marrow donor. But it didn't, and the treatments stopped working after a while. At least that's what I heard Mom telling one of her friends once."

"Your mother said they only had you to save him?"

"Well, no, she didn't actually say that, but it's what she meant. Patrick was perfect, and all I ever did was get in trouble. I got in trouble at school for not paying attention. The teachers said I liked to daydream too much. And then the thing with Derek. It's like I always disappoint Mom."

"What about your dad?" he asked. I could feel him staring at the side of my face, but I couldn't look at him.

"Same thing. I always disappoint him. He loves to swim, so he tried to teach me like he did Patrick, but I never got the hang of it. He said to me, 'Kincaid, this doesn't have to be so hard. Your brother could swim like a fish.' I really tried, Joseph, but I was scared I would drown and be dead like Patrick. Dad loves science, too, and had all these science experiment kits leftover from when Patrick was alive. He tried to share them with me, but science isn't my thing. No matter how hard I try, even with tutoring, I can't seem to get a grade higher than a 'C.' They've got a freaking shrine to him in our living room. I have to walk past the wall of photos of him every day on my way to school—a constant reminder that I'll never be as perfect as he was. So, I stopped trying to be perfect. I dyed my hair so it wouldn't be the same color as Patrick's was before he lost it, and my parents didn't even care enough to yell at me about it."

Joseph didn't say anything for a few minutes; he just looked out at the parking lot, and I began to wonder if I'd said too much. Then he took my hand and held it on top of my knee. "I'm sorry," he said. "Not just now, but for before when I teased you about your hair."

"It's okay." I stood up. "Can we walk over to the playground?"

He got up and followed me. "No, it isn't okay," he said. "You were just trying to get your parents to notice you, and I made fun of you for it. I was a jerk."

We walked over to the swings and sat down, much like we had the first day we'd met.

"You told me I was pretty at the same time you insulted my hair," I teased. "Clown-college drop-out? That's a playground insult if I've ever heard one."

He sighed. "I make stupid jokes when I'm nervous. I forgot for a minute what my parents taught me about not judging people by what they look like. You are pretty, though."

Relieved he couldn't see me blushing in the moonlight, I hoped he would open up to me since he'd mentioned his parents. I wasn't ready to tell him about my parents' troubled marriage. "Do you miss them a lot—your parents?" He nodded and looked away again. "I can't imagine mine not being there anymore even when they're…"

I couldn't finish my thought. No matter how much my parents drove me crazy, I couldn't imagine losing them as a teenager.

"It was cold the night they died." Joseph's voice was soft, and the air around us grew silent as if even the tree frogs and crickets had stopped to listen. I reached for his hand and held it, not knowing if it was the right thing to do. "Two days after New Year's Day. It was raining on and off all day, but not really sleeting much. A few degrees colder and it would've been, I think. My parents and Veronica were going to a dinner party, but I didn't want to go, so I came over here to help your grandpa with a leak in one of the rooms. He was going to drive me home since school was starting back the next day after the holiday break.

"Somehow, my dad skidded off the road, hit something and flipped over several times before they crashed. The police said it was probably black ice from freezing rain. Mom and Dad died instantly, and Veronica was thrown from the car. She had to have surgery to reduce the pressure on her brain and to repair her broken arm. She almost died on the table and once more in ICU before they got her stabilized. She stayed in the hospital for more than two weeks. When she woke up, she had to deal with the death of our parents and the shock of losing all her long hair.

"It's completely crazy, but one of the police officers who worked the accident told Sylvia that Veronica was a rare exception because if she had been wearing her seatbelt, she would've died too. My sister always wore her seatbelt. Every single time she got in a car. It's a miracle she forgot that night."

He was holding my hand so tightly at that point, I couldn't feel my fingers, but I didn't dare move. I wanted him to keep talking. Things were different between us already. We'd gone from strangers to friends so quickly I didn't think either of us had noticed when our relationship changed.

"And the scariest part was that there was a fence post right through the seat I would've sat in," Joseph continued. "I went to the scrap yard and saw the car, even though I probably shouldn't have. There's no way I could have survived the accident if I'd been with them."

"Wow," I said. His story gave me chills.

Joseph stood, walked over to the picnic table, and sat down with his back to me. "Veronica is the only family I have left. When she was in the hospital, I prayed more than I ever had for her to live. I had it in my head that if she died, I would kill myself because I didn't think I could make it on my own without her. I still dream about them sometimes, so vividly, like everything's okay. Like Dad and I are out looking at the stars with my telescope like we used to. It was one of his favorite things to do. Then I wake up and remember that it's not, and it might never be. But each time, I feel like my mom was just there, giving me a hug like she used to when I was a little boy and had bad dreams."

"Joseph…" I walked up behind him and placed my hand on his back.

He turned to me. "I hope God and my parents forgive me for wanting to give up like that. I know there's hope, and I'll have my own family someday, but I still feel really guilty for thinking that way. Don't tell anyone, okay? I haven't told anyone else."

My heart hurt for him, and tears welled up in my eyes. I reached out to touch his cheek and felt tears on my fingertips. I hadn't realized he was crying. I did the only thing I could; I stepped forward and hugged him the same way he had hugged me the day before and promised him I wouldn't tell a soul. He hugged me back and didn't let go for a while. I'd never wanted to kiss anyone so badly, and I didn't even know his last name.

Lesson 13: *It's much sadder and more contagious when boys cry.*

Chapter 12

The next morning, I stayed in bed as late as I could. Eventually, I had to get up and get ready for church with my grandparents. The only times I'd set foot in a church were when I went with them as a little kid. I usually didn't care if I went or not, but seeing Joseph again was on my mind. I wanted to know he was okay. My feelings of maybe liking him had gone to definitely liking him within the span of one conversation.

Wearing the only church-worthy outfit I'd brought with me—a sundress with yellow sunflowers on it—I fixed my hair, put in my contacts and put on a little makeup. The pink in my hair had faded to barely noticeable, and I wasn't sure if I wanted to dye it again. It had faded more in the last week than it had during the first three. Most of the time, I hadn't even thought about it until I passed by a mirror or saw my reflection in a window.

I took my Discman with me and listened to my copy of Nirvana's *Unplugged* album during the drive to church, playing Joseph's favorite song, "Pennyroyal Tea," over and over again, thinking it would bring me closer to him somehow. Lost in my daydreams, I didn't even realize we'd arrived at the church until the car skidded to a stop in the gravel parking lot of the blond brick building. There was a cemetery to the left behind a chain-link fence.

"You ready?" Grandpa asked. "It'll be a big crowd today for Father's Day."

Crap, I hadn't remembered. "Happy Father's Day, Grandpa," I said as we got out of the car. "I guess I need to call Dad later."

"You should," Grandpa said.

"Poor Joe," Grandma said, looking off in the distance. I followed her gaze and saw Joseph putting red flowers on a grave out in the middle of the cemetery.

"He'll be all right," Grandpa said. "The first ones are always the hardest, but he got through Mother's Day okay. He'll be strong for this one too."

"I'm going to wait for Joseph since he invited me here," I said. "Is that okay? I'll see you inside." My grandparents went inside, and I stood by the fence for a moment, debating on if I should go in the cemetery or if it was more of a private moment for Joseph. I ultimately decided to go to him after waiting a couple of minutes.

Carefully avoiding the graves, I followed the dirt path to where Joseph was standing. He turned to me as I walked up. "Hey," he said, with little expression on his face.

"Hey," I said, looking down at the grave. Bennett. The double-stone read: *Ronald and Diana Bennett, January 3, 1995.* "Father's Day's tough, huh?" I couldn't believe I just said something so stupid and wanted to kick myself. Joseph nodded and turned back to the graves. "Joseph Bennett…"

He turned back to me and smiled a little. "That's me."

"Kincaid Walsh." I stuck my hand out for him to shake. "Nice to meet you."

Joseph chuckled at my silly introduction and took my hand. "I think we're past the 'nice to meet you' stage, aren't we?" he asked.

"I didn't know your last name until now."

"And you'll never get to meet my parents," he said, gesturing toward the graves. "So here they are. They always liked meeting my friends. I think they would've liked you."

"I would've liked to have met them." The eye contact with him was so intense, I thought about kissing him right there in the cemetery but figured it would be bad timing.

"Come on," he said, taking my hand again as bells began ringing from the church. "The service is about to start." He held my hand until we reached the front steps and then opened the door for me.

People were singing when we walked in and joined his friends in the balcony. Amy and Dustin moved down to make room for us, and Heather and Kevin waved at me. Joseph handed me a hymnal and opened it to the page they were singing from. I read along with the words while everyone sang, trying to take it all in. I could pick out individual voices from below that were off-key and ones near me—like Amy—that were perfect, yet all blended together with the organ at the front of the church in close-enough harmony.

The words were like no poetry I'd ever read—full of unwavering faith and lacking fear.

Lesson 14: Hymns are poetry.

By the time the sermon started, I felt refreshed and ready to listen. In honor of Father's Day, the pastor talked about God being the ultimate father and thanked the

Earthly fathers and father-figures for doing the hardest job there was.

I thought about my own father and what he might be doing. I'd had good times with him, too, not just fights. He was the ultimate monster-killer when I was five, always willing to check under the bed or in the closet one more time after my mother had lost her patience with me not wanting to go to bed. Where was that guy now, and who was the guy who barely looked at me when he said goodbye a week ago? I wondered if he'd even want to talk to me on the phone later.

Grandma and Grandpa tried to get Joseph to come home with us for lunch after the service since Veronica wouldn't be home until the evening, but he already had lunch plans with Kevin and his family. It was hard for me to remember to breathe as I said goodbye to him. It was impossible for me to be in love with him so soon, but we were closer now, and something would happen between us. I could just feel it.

After lunch, I called my dad. I had to wait a few minutes for him to get to the phone since there were no phones in the individual rooms at the retreat location. I tried to figure out what to talk to him about.

"Hey, sweetheart," he said. "How are you liking your summer break so far?"

"Hi, Dad." I started to tell him about meeting Eduardo Martinez, but then I lost control of my mouth. "How's the marriage-saving retreat?" Dead silence. "Is it working?"

"Kincaid…"

"Sylvia told me. She assumed I already knew. Why didn't you and Mom tell me? I'm not a child." Angry tears stung in my eyes.

"We didn't tell you because you are a child, Kincaid," he said. "And it's our job to protect you and keep you safe." He always spoke redundantly when he was frustrated with me. "Your mother and I love you very much and want what's best for you."

"What if what's best for me is for you two to love each other?"

"We do love each other, and we always will."

"Uh-huh."

"Do you want to talk to Mom? Maybe she can explain everything better."

"No. I just called to wish you a Happy Father's Day. I'm done talking." I slammed down the phone before he could say anything else. I tuned the clock radio to a loud station and fell back on the bed, blocking out the light with my arms.

What was so difficult about staying together? You fall in love, get married, and live happily ever after. Sure, some bad stuff happens along the way, but you're supposed to get through it together, not give up on each other and break up your family. They'd been together for twenty-five years, since they were teenagers. Wasn't a quarter-century too much time invested to just throw everything away? I vowed then that I would do anything in the world to make sure my marriage didn't fall apart someday.

After some annoying tears and a nap, I got up and washed my face. I put on my glasses rather than putting my contacts back in and went to the apartment. My grandparents had a card table set up in the corner and were working on the largest jigsaw puzzle I'd ever seen.

"It keeps our minds sharp," Grandpa said, holding up one of the tiny pieces.

"Pull up a chair and join us, dear," Grandma said.

I did as she asked and started working on a portion of the puzzle, which was a scene of a sunset with a lighthouse. The task, which I thought would be tedious, proved to be relaxing. After working in silence for a while, Grandma wanted to talk.

"They called it 'courting' in our day," she said.

"What do you mean?"

Grandpa chuckled. "She means what you kids call 'dating' or 'hanging out' these days—what our kids called 'going steady.'"

"Oh." I wondered where the conversation was going.

"I had to go ask Grandma's father's permission to court her. We went on some chaperoned dates until she was sixteen when we were finally allowed to go to a movie theater or a soda shop by ourselves. That was 1939, a couple of years before the war. I was eighteen then, twenty when I enlisted, right after we got married."

"And so handsome in your uniform," Grandma interjected. "You were the handsomest man around, and you still make my heart flutter."

Grandpa took her hand from across the table and kissed it. "As does mine, dear." They were so cute. Why couldn't my parents be like that? Had they ever been? "Joe's sweet on you, Kincaid."

"Oh, he is," Grandma said. "I've never seen him so happy than when we agreed to let you go to the movies with him Friday night. That poor boy has been through so much. He's such a good boy, so polite and helpful."

They were practically pushing me into Joseph's arms. A vast difference to how my parents would react if they knew how I felt about him. "He's nice, Grandma," I said, trying to control my blushing. "I think we'll be good friends."

"Did he talk to you about what happened with his family?" she asked. It's like she was psychic all of a sudden.

"Grandpa did. But Joseph told me a little too. It's really sad."

"Did you call your father?" Grandpa asked, handing me a puzzle piece that matched my section. "Sylvia told us she spilled the beans to you about what's going on with your parents."

"Yeah, I called him."

"How's your mother?"

"I didn't talk to her, Grandpa."

"Marriage is hard work, Kincaid," Grandma said. "Don't be too hard on your mother. She loves you."

"I know." But did she love me as much as she'd loved Patrick? I wasn't sure Grandma could answer that question. I didn't think anyone could, not even my mother.

Chapter 13

After I'd had as much of the puzzle and conversation as I could stand, I grabbed my notebook out of my room and headed to the docks to write, hoping there wouldn't be a huge crowd of guests by the lake. I didn't get that lucky. There were several families playing on the bank and some going out in boats from the newest dock. I just wanted some peace and quiet outside my room.

I noticed an older dock farther down the lake, away from the swimming area. It was unoccupied, so I walked over the rocks to get there. I put on Joseph's baseball cap to block out the sun and opened my notebook. I'd had a poem churning around in my mind since Joseph had shared his secret with me, so I wanted to get it down on paper before I forgot it. I turned to a blank page at the end of my lessons and began writing.

I scribbled things out and rearranged passages until I was happy with it. Everything that flowed out was my interpretation of Joseph's feelings.

"The Night" A poem by Kincaid Walsh

Deep in the night I had a dream, and in it everything was okay.
I was thoroughly happy, and nothing could take that away from me.
I wasn't at all doubtful, and in fact, feeling that way was entirely unknown to me.
Everything worked out for the better the first time through, and it always had.

Deep in the night I had a dream, and in it everything was not okay.
Beauty was not in the eyes of the beholder, and I couldn't find it in me.
I was afraid of everything, and nothing would take that away from me.
All I wanted was for someone to take away my pain,
and that person could have been me.

Deep in the night I had a dream, and in it everything was so real.
I can't say I was always happy, and I won't say that I was always sad.
I found true beauty in the most unnoticed places, and one of those places held me.
Everything happened for a reason, and it all made perfect sense somewhere.

Deep in the night I realized that this dream was only a dream, and at once I smiled.
My mother's love was in my heart, and she wasn't far away from me.
My father's love was in my eyes, and he was in the stars watching over me.
I could almost feel the love of a future family and see them surrounding me.

Deep in the night I woke up, and knew, that both the night and the dream were forever a part of me.

"Nature is the best environment for writing," Eduardo Martinez said from the back of the dock, startling me. He was carrying a small folding chair. "Do you mind if I join you?"

I stood up to greet him. "Of course not, Mr. Martinez. I was working on some poetry."

"You can call me Ed." He set up his chair as I sat on the dock again. "It's beautiful here. A lot calmer than the ocean's shore."

"I've never seen the ocean, but I want to someday."

"Everyone should see the ocean before they die," Ed said. "What kind of poetry do you write? I always had an affinity for love poetry with concrete details. At least that's what all those poetry analysts at all the universities told me."

"My poetry is more abstract, I guess. I haven't had any real training, but I've heard I need to use more concrete details like in your poems."

He put his hand out toward my notebook. "May I?" I handed it to him and waited with bated breath while he read it. He stroked the beginnings of a goatee on his chin and handed the notebook back to me. I was terrified to ask him what he thought. "You know who else has never had any real training for poetry?"

"Who?" I asked as I looked down at the writing in my notebook.

"Me."

"Really?" With his perfect lines, I figured he'd had years of training.

"Really." He pulled a tiny leather-bound book out of his shirt pocket and handed it to me. "Look at the first page."

I opened it and read my favorite poem in his messy cursive writing with scribbles and rearranged words.

Summer roses baking in the sun
or illuminated in the moonlight
envy your great beauty, my dear love.

Birds from farthest north
and butterflies stop to let you pass,
reveling in your grace, my dear love.

Brooks change their direction
and storms dissipate their wrath
to please you, my dear love.

Wars end and begin again
unlike my love for you, my dear.
I'll build you a life stronger than any wall
if you'll hold me and keep me near, my dear.

My jaws ached from smiling so much while I read it. "This is my favorite poem in the world," I told him. He grinned at me. "I can't believe you carry it around with you like this."

"I didn't even know it was a poem when I wrote it. I sent that to Rosa in a letter when I asked her to marry me during the war. She saved all of my letters. I wrote it in my notebook first to get it right."

"It's beautiful. I love all your poetry, but this one just makes me feel and see how much you loved her. I want someone to love me that much someday." And I wanted to love someone so much. If it could also be the same person who loved me, it would be divine. "I think it would be amazing to be someone's favorite author or poet someday."

"I'm no great poet," he said. "I'm just an ordinary man who happened to fall in love with an extraordinary woman. The only way I could communicate with her was through poetry because my voice disappeared, and I felt weak in the knees when I was in the presence of her stunning beauty. A young man will feel that way about you someday; I'm sure of it. He'll let you see his vulnerability and give you a piece of his soul if you'll do the same. But grant him the courtesy of letting him die first so he won't have to live without you. I miss my Rosa every minute of every day. She could make even the darkest days seem bright again."

Joseph had already shown vulnerability when he cried in front of me. Hearing Ed describe Rosa was gut-wrenching. I wanted to bring her back to life for him. "I'm so sorry for your loss," I said. But saying it wasn't enough. Nothing I could say was.

"Get writing training, Kincaid. Or don't. But whatever you do, don't let someone tell you that you're not already a writer. The poem you just shared with me is full of thought-provoking emotion and truth, hopes, and dreams—exactly what writing should be. You're a good writer. Who cares if it lacks concrete details the so-called experts want? There are writing and poetry rules for folks who need them, but rules can always be broken."

"I feel like I'm always breaking the rules, especially when I'm writing poetry," I told him. "I want to write a novel someday that makes people laugh and cry and feel things they haven't been able to describe in words before—until they read my work. I dream about it, like when I read *To Kill a Mockingbird*, *A Separate Peace*, or *The Catcher in the Rye*."

"Writers are like musicians. There are the ones who are self-taught out of passion that never learn how to read music. They play from their hearts. Then there are those who take lessons to learn all the techniques and read music. Maybe they love it, and maybe they don't. Maybe they become great masters of their art in the process, but if that passion isn't there, it's just a monotonous cycle of mediocrity. I'd rather break every single one of the rules and stay true to my heart than follow them all and be a shell of a person."

We sat in silence for another hour, both of us scribbling in our notebooks, occasionally looking up to watch a duck swim by. Friends had told me before that I was a good writer, but after hearing it from Eduardo Martinez, I could float all the way up to the stars and never come down again.

Lesson 15: Compliments that come from the right person at the right time can change everything.

My phone was ringing when I got back to my room, and I ran to answer it.

"Kincaid!" Courtney said. "Where the hell have you been? I've been calling you for the last few days."

"I'm sorry, Court!" I flopped down on the bed. "I have so much to tell you."

"About Joseph?"

"That and other things." I turned over on my back, restricted by the length of the cord.

She squealed. "Spill it, girl!"

"Todd tried to help me learn how to swim on Friday afternoon…"

"Kincaid, no! I thought you were going to stay away from him. He's too old for you!"

"It was innocent, Courtney. He thinks I'm a kid, and he's sleeping with Joseph's sister, anyway."

"Oh?"

"Different story. Anyway, it was kind of hurtful the way he told Veronica I was just a little girl after she scolded him about being careful around me. I went back to my room, and Joseph was there. He asked me if I wanted to go into town with him and could tell I was upset. I don't know what happened, but I couldn't stop myself from crying in front of him."

"Oh, my God! How did he react to that?"

"He was so sweet, Court. He hugged me."

"That is sweet," she said as loud music started in the background. "My bratty little sister is trying to listen through the door. Now she can't hear me. Go on!"

I told Courtney everything about my "maybe date" with Joseph, and she agreed it sounded like a real date, considering his actions at the movie, his friends' comments in the restroom, and the kiss on the cheek. She thought purity-pledge teenagers in relationships usually got closer to having sex than us regular virgins because they would find technical ways to be close without actually going all the way. When I told her about Sylvia's description of her first time, Courtney was as horrified.

Keeping Joseph's tearful confession private was more important to me than dishing to my best friend, so I skipped over that and dished about meeting Eduardo Martinez instead. I'd analyzed so many of his poems for class assignments, Courtney was probably sick to death of hearing about him, but she listened graciously and really perked up when I talked about sitting with Joseph at church.

Courtney filled me in on all the things happening in our town—who was going out and who had broken up. She didn't mention Derek, and I didn't ask. He was the last thing on my mind. I wanted to talk to Joseph again.

"I'm so jealous that you basically already have a boyfriend this summer," she said. "No one thinks of me that way."

"You'll find the right one. There's something else I need to tell you, but you can't tell anyone—none of our other friends. Promise."

"I promise, geez, Kincaid. You know I can keep a secret." She pulled away from the phone. "Get away from my door, squirt, or I'm telling Dad!"

"Is she gone?" I asked, annoyed for her about her sister's attempted spying.

"Yeah."

"My parents might be getting a divorce."

The phone dropped. Courtney scrambled to pick it up again and bombarded me with questions. "Holy shit! Are you okay? What's going to happen? Who are you going to live with? Do you have to move and go to a different school? Oh, my God, Kincaid! I'm so sorry."

"Geez, Court," I said, sitting up. "Slow down. I don't know anything yet."

"What do you know?"

I told her everything I knew, and she reminded me that having a stepparent wasn't so bad. Of course, her situation was different than mine. Something Courtney didn't like to talk about was the fact that her mother was in prison and would be for several years. From what I'd read in the newspaper archives at the library, Courtney's mom had been caught up in an embezzling scheme at her former employer. Several people had gone to prison over it. Courtney's dad had been remarried for years, long enough to bring ten-year-old Mauve into their family. They also had an older brother who lived on his own.

We had other friends whose parents were divorced. Being split between two households sounded the worst to me. I liked having only one room with all my books and stuff in one place. But there was no sense worrying about it since I didn't know for sure what would happen. Courtney agreed it was better to forget about it until I knew something definite so I could focus my time on developing a relationship with Joseph.

After she hung up, I thought about Joseph and something I hadn't considered before. He lived six hours away from me. Even if he did want to be my boyfriend, it would never work out because we would only get to see each other during the summer and school breaks when I could visit my grandparents.

If my parents divorced, Dad would stay in our hometown because his plumbing business was established there. I could live with him and finish school with my friends. Mom worked at a bank and could transfer anywhere or find a job at a different bank. Would she move here to be close to her parents? If she did, and I lived with her, I would have to leave my friends, but I would have new ones ready and waiting with Joseph and the kids from his church. He could be my boyfriend then, but I didn't want to wish for it if it meant my parents splitting up. But deep down, I did wish for Joseph to be my boyfriend. I'd realized it while talking to Courtney.

I turned on MTV to drown out the noise in my head and fell asleep listening to the music videos that became a soundtrack to my dreams.

Chapter 14

Mondays were the hardest days for Veronica and Sylvia because so many guests checked out after the weekends. They had twelve rooms to clean before three o'clock check-in, and only half of those guests had checked out early. Grandma and Grandpa asked me to take a break from the fence to help get the rooms ready.

After breakfast, I took the yellow rubber gloves Grandma had given me and found my aunt standing on the porch waiting for me. "You ready?" she asked.

"I guess so. What do you want me to do?"

"I thought I would put you on stripping the sheets and pillows off the beds first, then you can help put new ones on after we disinfect the mattresses and pillows. All the rooms that need cleaning have the doors propped open, so get started, please."

Gross. Disinfecting mattresses and dirty sheets. But I figured it was better than cleaning the bathrooms. I went to the first room and stripped the bed, dragging the sheets and bedspreads out to the separate carts on the sidewalk and continued on to the next room. By the time I had three rooms done, I was sweating.

Veronica came in carrying a bucket while I was stripping the fourth bed. "Wow," she said. "You're a fast worker."

I shrugged. "Just doing what Sylvia asked." I thought she looked older as I studied her face, unsure if it was the day's or the weekend's events that had caused it. I was dying to ask her about it, but I didn't know her well enough to utter a word.

She noticed me looking at her. "What is it?" she asked, puzzled by my inability to look away. "Oh. You're still freaked out about what your aunt told us, aren't you?"

I bit my lip and nodded. "Maybe a little."

Veronica walked over to me and spoke quietly. "I don't think everyone's first time is like Sylvia's," she said, looking me in the eye. She lowered her voice to speak in a whisper. "Mine wasn't that bad. But you should wait until you're older." She smirked at me. "Especially since my little brother has a thing for you. He said y'all had fun at the movies Friday."

I turned away to hide my red cheeks and continued struggling with the sheets.

"He's kind of sensitive," she continued as she sprayed cleaner on a rag and wiped the nightstand and the phone. "But don't tell him I told you that or he'll kill me."

I had to get her to stop talking about Joseph and me. "How long have you been with Todd?"

Veronica sat down in the armchair. "I guess Joe's told you about our parents." I nodded and sat on the bed. "I met Todd at the hospital after the accident. He was volunteering there and helping a friend of his with some burn and physical therapy at the same time I was there. We started talking and became friends. He helped me with some of my schoolwork for my GED. I was in my senior year when the accident happened, so I figured I'd still finish on time if I took the test. Anyway, I found out Todd would be working here for the summer and started dating him right after I passed my test in April."

"So, you've only been dating him for two months?"

97

"I don't think the length of time matters as much as the connection," she said, standing again with her bucket. "The bathroom's calling me. Ugh."

Lesson 16: The length of time you know someone doesn't matter as much as the connection.

By the time I finished stripping the beds in the first six rooms, I was exhausted. I still had time to strip the remaining rooms before my lunch break. I was amazed at the sheer volume of the laundry shoved into the carts. I didn't think Grandma's laundry room could handle it all.

"We can't wash all that here," Sylvia said with a laugh when I asked about the laundry. "Only the sheets can be washed here. We have to take the bedspreads to the laundromat in town. Joe's supposed to take care of it later this afternoon."

I hoped she would send me with him, which I guess was obvious on my face. She and Veronica glanced at each other as they put new linens on the bed and started laughing.

"Yes, Kaykay," Sylvia said. "You can go with him if it's okay with Grandma and Grandpa."

I rolled the cart of laundry to the apartment and got Grandma's permission to go with Joseph to help him at the laundromat. She handed me a roll of quarters and some laundry detergent and sent me on my way.

After stopping by my room to wash my face and put on new makeup, I headed to the playground to find Joseph. I heard Grandpa and Ed's voices as I approached the gate.

"I can't imagine having to go on without Darla," Grandpa said. "I don't know how you go on without Rosa, Ed."

"One day at a time, Chester," Ed said. "One day at a time. It's easier being here than waking up at our house without her there. At least, here, I can pretend I'm still a young man taking a trip for work."

Joseph's voice made me stop in my tracks. "How did you know you loved your wives before you married them?" he asked.

Grandpa chuckled. "I'd known her since we were kids in church, skipping stones and going fishing with the other kids," he said. "Then one day, when I was about fifteen or so, it hit me like a ton of bricks that she was damn well the prettiest girl I'd ever seen. She was only thirteen at the time, so we had to wait until we were older before we could court officially, but I did steal a kiss once before then."

"Smooth operator," Ed said. "My Rosa stopped my heart for a moment when I first saw her. I couldn't even speak in her presence for a couple of months. I had to write everything down."

"Shouldn't it be easy?" Joseph asked. "Like, if you trust her?"

"It gets that way sooner or later," Grandpa said. "Especially after you get past your nerves long enough to get that first kiss out of the way."

Ed started laughing, followed by Grandpa. I didn't hear Joseph, so I took that as my cue to interrupt them. Joseph noticed me right away and stood up at the picnic table. Grandpa and Ed were playing chess together at the table under the shade tree.

"H-Hey, Kincaid," Joseph stammered. "Where'd you come from?"

Ed looked at Joseph and me. "Youngsters," he said. "Feels like I was that young only yesterday." He turned back to Grandpa and laughed.

Joseph walked over to me. "I missed working with you this morning," he said. "Did you get finished with everything?"

"The bedspreads need to be washed," I said, holding up the roll of quarters. "There are twelve of them today."

"Oh, yeah, I guess I better go do that."

"Grandma said I could go with you to help out. If you want me to."

"Have you eaten?" he asked. I shook my head. "Let's get something to eat while the bedspreads wash. There's a burger place right next door. It'll be a good way to pass the time."

We piled the dirty bedspreads into large plastic tubs in the back of his truck and drove into town. At the laundromat, I helped him shove two bedspreads in each of the six largest front-loading washing machines I'd ever seen. After we'd started them all, I stood hypnotized as I watched them fill with soap and water and start spinning around, slow at first, then going faster and faster.

"Let's go eat," Joseph said, knocking me out of my washer-induced trance. "It'll be almost an hour before the laundry's done, and then we'll still have to wait for it to dry."

He opened the door for me and led me next door to a hole-in-the-wall diner that felt like we had stepped back in time to the 1950s. The waitresses were on roller-skates—a sight that made me laugh.

"Just sit anywhere, Joe!" one of the skating waitresses called. "I'll be right with you."

"They know you here?" I asked as we sat in one of the booths.

"I come here with my friends sometimes, and when I have to go to the laundromat for your grandma. She says it hurts her arthritis to pull the heavy bedspreads out of the washer, so I started doing it for her. I do most of the laundry at home now, anyway. Someone had to."

I knew of no other teenage boys who did laundry. "What else do you do?"

"Cleaning, mowing, trash, what maintenance I can, and about half the cooking. We have a small vegetable garden Veronica deals with, and she does a lot of the cleaning and the other half of the cooking. It works for us. We always had chores; it's just...now they're amplified."

"My mom just now started letting me help with the laundry since she's finally convinced I won't screw it up."

"Have you talked to them—your parents? I know you were pretty upset with them."

The waitress skated over and interrupted us. "You want your usual, hon?" She ruffled Joseph's hair.

"Yes, ma'am," he said.

"And for you, miss?" she asked. I skimmed the menu and ordered a BLT. "Excellent choice. One ticket?"

"Yes," Joseph said before I could answer her.

"Joseph," I said as the waitress walked away.

"I can afford to buy you a three-dollar sandwich." His face was red as he picked up a dessert menu. "And there's even dessert here."

"It's not that," I said.

"Then what is it?" he said, his lips a fine line as he looked up at me. "Veronica's constantly on my ass about living a little, having fun, and not saving every penny I earn. I can spend my money however I want to, and I want to buy you lunch."

I hadn't meant to offend him. "Don't you remember at the movies when you said I could pay the next time we went out? Isn't this next time?"

The irritation melted from his face. "I'm sorry," he said. "I'm a jerk. I get a little sensitive about money, and I shouldn't have taken it out on you. I asked you here, so I thought I'd pay."

"Technically, I invited myself along on your work trip. You can pay next time."

"So, there will still be a next time?" he asked, reaching for my hand across the table.

"I hope so." I squeezed his hand. "I like hanging out with you."

We talked about upcoming movies for the summer that we wanted to see while we waited for our food, which came out surprisingly quick. Halfway through the meal, I shared my secret about what was going on with my parents. His expression changed from a warm smile to concern as I spoke.

"I'm so sorry, Kincaid."

"I guess I'll just have to deal with it. Now that I think back about the last year or so, even before I got in trouble, they got to where they didn't fight anymore, at least not in front of me. They stopped talking for the most part."

"Maybe the retreat will help them remember why they fell in love in the first place," he suggested. "Maybe you're worrying for no reason."

But there was a reason; I just knew it. "But what if it's not for no reason?"

"Then you'll get through it."

"I'd have to decide who to live with. Probably my mom. Grandma told her she could move here."

Joseph tried to stifle a smile that left his jaw tight. "That wouldn't be the worst thing in the world, would it?"

"I'd miss my friends and my dad, but ...I guess you're right; it wouldn't be horrible. I'd know you and your friends at school."

"They wouldn't just be my friends, Kincaid, they'd be your friends too," he said, moving over to sit beside me. "All of them liked you when we went out on Friday, and they were glad to get to see you again at church yesterday. And I like you."

I kissed him on the cheek as he had after our date, taking him by surprise. "I like you, too, Joseph." When I looked up, Heather was walking toward us, dressed in ballet gear with a small bag thrown over her shoulder. That explained her bun on Friday; she probably had a class that day. I'd never been friends with an actual ballerina before.

"Hey, guys," she said. "Do you mind if I sit for a minute? My mom had to drop me off a little early for class."

"Sure," Joseph said. "We're waiting on motel laundry."

"I'm so nervous," she said, looking over her shoulder at the door. "Kevin and I find out today what parts we got in *The Nutcracker*. The auditions were last week, and I've been a nervous wreck ever since."

"You'll get a good part," Joseph said. "You always do."

The waitress skated over with a look of concern and set a glass of water in front of Heather. "I promise I'll come back after class and get a milkshake," Heather said with a smile. The waitress nodded and skated away. Heather turned and looked at me. "She thinks I'm too skinny, but I swear I eat like a horse after class."

The bell dinged on the front door, and Kevin came in wearing tights, a tank top, and athletic shorts. He was missing the earrings, eyeliner, and nail polish from Friday night, and his hair was slicked back into a small ponytail. Several of the other customers turned to look at him and then went back to eating or talking. He rushed over to our table. "You're looking at the Nutcracker Prince," he said.

"Really? That's awesome, babe!" Heather said, standing up. "I need to check the roster."

"Couldn't have done it without you, my 'Clara,'" he said. Heather squealed and kissed him on the lips, gaining the attention of everyone in the diner. Kevin announced their news to everyone. "My amazing girlfriend just got one of the lead parts in *The Nutcracker*." Everyone applauded our dancing friends as they left the diner.

I turned to Joseph. "Okay, I will definitely come back here for their performance."

"I'll see you there," he said with a grin.

Chapter 15

When Joseph and I got back to the motel with the laundry, Grandma was sitting on the porch talking on the phone, its long cord stretched through the open screen door. She waved me over and shoved the phone into my hands.

"It's your mother," she said. "Talk to her."

I figured the repercussions of the conversation with my father would come back to bite me eventually, but I wasn't expecting it at that moment. Especially while standing in front of Joseph. I waved at him and took the phone back inside, closing the door behind me. "Hi, Mom," I said into the receiver. "How are you?"

"I should be asking you that," she said. "I've been talking to your grandma, and apparently, I've missed a lot going on in your life. Joseph, for example. I thought we agreed you were too young for a boyfriend."

I sat down at the card table and looked at the puzzle pieces strewn about. "No, Mom, you agreed, not me. And Joseph isn't my boyfriend; he's just a friend. Grandma and Grandpa know him from church and gave me permission to hang out with him."

"In a group," she said. "I think you're too young to spend time alone with him."

"Mom, do you not trust me at all?"

"It's just…" She sighed. "There are girls your age getting pregnant, and—"

"Geez, Mom!" I thumped a puzzle piece into the floor and stretched to retrieve it.

"I don't want that to be you."

"Well, Joseph is a card-carrying member of the virgin club at church, so you needn't worry about us."

"Kincaid, don't be brash."

"What, Mom? You worry I might sleep around and get pregnant at fifteen, but the word 'virgin' makes you uncomfortable? We were at the laundromat, which is not exactly romantic."

"Watch your tone…"

"You're the one who dumped me off here," I said. "I'm trying to make the best of it, but you can't expect me to sit around here away from my friends for the summer and not have anyone my own age to talk to, even if—God forbid—we happen to talk about sex even though you'd rather pretend it doesn't exist."

"Kincaid…"

"I get it. You don't like to talk about it. But I've already told you, I'm not having any. Mom, I like Joseph, and he likes me too. I want to see him."

"You're still a child."

"Yeah, but not so naïve that I don't know sex is complicated. Apparently, it's complicated even when you're married."

I thought she might have hung up on me, but then I heard her breathing. "I'm sorry I wasn't more open with you," she said. "About everything. Your father and I are still trying to work some things out."

"I don't want to keep you from it. Goodbye."

"Kincaid…"

"Do I have to stop seeing Joseph?" She didn't answer me. "Mom?"

"Kincaid, I love you," she said softly.

"I love you both." I hung up the phone and stared at the almost-finished puzzle that lay before me. I wished it were a portal I could walk right through to the ocean's shore and climb on top of the lighthouse to see where Earth ended.

Later that evening, Ed and I sat on the dock and discussed poetry and novels we'd read while my grandparents dozed in their recliners and Sylvia watched the office. It felt like I was still in school while talking to Ed—but only the best parts of it. I hadn't read a novel since school had let out, and I craved one. I figured Joseph would be willing to take me to the library soon. Technically, Mom hadn't answered me when I asked if I had to stop seeing him, which I took as the go-ahead to continue things as they were.

Late in the morning on Tuesday, I helped Grandma make apple jelly in her kitchen. Doing so made me feel like a little girl again, back when I thought she was the most impressive person alive—before I realized she had flaws like the rest of us. I was happy to help her, but I had to admit I missed painting with Joseph, who I knew was working without me.

"Did you have a good talk with your mother the other day?" she asked.

"Something like that," I said. "She was upset about me seeing Joseph."

"She'll come around. She forgets that she was barely fifteen when she first met your father."

I scoffed. "And look how well that's worked out."

"Love isn't always enough," Grandma said, handing me some boxes of gelatin. "Start opening those."

I did as she asked and helped her mix it with the liquid she poured off the apple peelings. She sat on a stool against the cabinets, bracing herself with her hands against the counter.

"Divorce doesn't necessarily mean they don't love each other anymore, either," she continued. "Losing a child changes a couple forever, and sometimes a marriage can't survive the pain of it, even if there is another child in the mix whom they love dearly and fiercely."

"It still hurts, though, Grandma."

"I know, child. I know." She dumped the boiled apple peelings into a bowl, the one she'd asked me to take outside later for the animals. She sat down again on her stool and started canning the jelly, letting me help her when I could. "There was a time when I hated apples and anything made from them."

"I didn't know that. You always have homemade applesauce in the freezer and apple jelly in your cupboard. Is it just because you have the apple trees on the property?"

"Part of the reason," she said. "Can't stand the thought of wasting food. During the Depression, there were times when all my family had to eat was apples or popcorn. My daddy's parents had the apple orchard, so when Daddy lost his job, and we lost our house, we moved to their land. We bartered for flour and lard and other necessities, and what apples we didn't use for pies or cobblers we turned into canned applesauce to preserve it. My grandmother taught me how to make apple jelly so we didn't waste the peels, and it became quite the luxury to have jelly for our bread throughout the winter. I never taught your mother how to make apple jelly because she was never interested, and your cousin, Sarah, lives even farther away than you. I know you probably aren't interested in the ramblings of an old lady, but I hope the jelly-making didn't bore you so."

"Of course not, Grandma. I love making jelly with you."

She smiled, though her eyes were wistful. "You'll have to write it down so you and your mother won't forget about me someday. She and I don't always view things the same way, but I love Susan. You and her will always have a home with me as long as I live, dear, no matter what happens with her marriage."

Even though I was several inches taller than Grandma, I felt so much smaller than her at that moment. She looked at me from her stool and frowned as she tried not to cry. I stopped what I was doing and hugged her, realizing for the first time how frail she felt in my arms. I had the horrifying realization that someday, maybe soon, I would have to live without her, like Ed had to live without Rosa. I wasn't sure Grandpa could survive the loss of Grandma.

"I love your father, too, Kincaid," she said, still in my arms. "But he's a shell of the man he once was since he lost your brother. I think both your parents are terrified of losing you, too, so don't let them. Keep loving them separately if they can't be together. Do it for me if for no one else."

I needed to apologize to my parents.

Lesson 17: Elders hold a wealth of wisdom.

After lunch and a quick greeting to Joseph as he left to buy more paint to finish the outside sections of the fence, I went to the dock hoping to find Ed. He was stretched out in his folding chair, throwing bread crumbs to the ducks surrounding him.

"They're never going to leave you alone, now," I said as I approached.

"I've always liked the coloring of ducks," Ed said. "Green and brown are the purest shades of nature. There aren't any ducks around my home in Colorado."

"When do you go back home?"

"Sometime after the Fourth. I'll have a long drive."

"Is it scary to drive all that way by yourself? I don't think I would like that very much."

"We don't always like what we have to do. It gets lonely on the road, wondering what your purpose is or your place in the universe. I'm planning to sell my house and travel for a while until I'm not able to anymore. I figure I've still got a few years before I'm not safe driving. Maybe I'll find my way back here to check up on you and your writing."

"I don't live here...yet," I said. Ed looked at me perplexed but didn't speak. He was waiting for me to explain. "There's a chance my parents are splitting up, and if that happens, I think my mom will move back here to be closer to her parents. I guess I would come with her."

"I'm sorry, Kincaid. I'm sure that's not a decision they'd enter into lightly. But, at the risk of sounding insensitive, there are a lot worse things in the world, like

111

what happened to your boyfriend. I bet if he could choose, he'd want his parents alive and apart if that were his only choice."

"Joseph's not my boyfriend, but I know what you mean."

He chuckled. "That boy has an artist's soul like you."

"I'm not sure what you mean."

"Your canvas is the page, your paint the written word," Ed said. "Joseph captures the beauty or pain around him on paper and canvas through drawing or painting. That's his chosen way of expression."

"I had no idea he drew," I said. "And I haven't seen him paint anything but the fence planks."

"He'll share that part of himself with you when he's ready." Ed went back to feeding the ducks, sighing a bit with each toss of the bread crumbs. "Talk to him about the meaning of the lake. Share your poetry with him."

I wanted so badly to see the artistic side of Joseph. He had offered to help me learn to swim, which would be the perfect opportunity to talk about the lake. "What if he laughs at my poetry?"

"Then I'll admit I misjudged the boy. As old as I am, though, I can smell bullshit from a mile away, and I think he'll be moved by your poem as much as I was—as much as other people will be when you share it with them."

"It's scary to share things. I haven't even shown my new writing to my parents or my best friend since I had a poem published in the school newspaper. I'm afraid they'll not like it or continue to think I'm weird for wanting to become a writer."

"There's no becoming a writer, Kincaid. It's just in your soul. You're born a writer. It's whether you choose to share it with others that makes them see it. You've got to have thick skin. The most important person who must love your writing is you. When someone else likes it, it's just a bonus. There'll be an audience for your work. Write for them and don't fret about anyone who doesn't like it. It ain't them you're writing for."

"I'm still scared."

Ed looked out at the water and groaned as he stretched. "It is scary, but promise me you'll share your work, Kincaid. Sharing love, fear, beauty, and pain helps non-artists make sense of it all—especially the pain."

I promised him, and then he spoke the words that stuck with me—my second lesson of the day.

Lesson 18: (courtesy of the great poet, Eduardo Martinez) Artists don't necessarily feel things more deeply than other people; they just have a way to express their pain so that it's universally understood.

Chapter 16

I was up early and already waiting for Joseph when he arrived to continue painting the fence. My eagerness to get started amused him until I explained I wanted to finish early so he could teach me to swim.

According to Joseph, I didn't need supervision anymore to paint the fence properly. Even so, we stayed close and worked together to get another section done before it got too hot to continue. The last thing I wanted was to puke again or get another sunburn.

I ate with my grandparents and helped them add a few more puzzle pieces while Joseph drove home to get his swim trunks and eat lunch. I went back to my room and looked at both of my swimsuit options, the bikini or the one-piece. Deciding to go with the practical choice, I slipped on the one-piece and fixed my hair in a bun. I took out my contacts and put on my glasses, which I planned to leave on the bank. I pulled on some shorts and grabbed my flip-flops as Joseph pulled into the parking lot.

As he stepped out of the truck, the sunlight hit him just right to take my breath away. I had no idea what I was thinking before about Todd; it was always Joseph I should have been watching, and he actually liked me.

Shirtless, he strolled over to me with his towel thrown over his shoulder. "You ready?" I nodded, unable to speak for a moment as I looked at him. "You need a towel, don't you?"

"Crap," I said, heading back into my room. "I knew I was forgetting something." I grabbed my towel off the bed and took a deep breath to slow my pounding heart.

Wednesday was a slow day for guests, so there was only one older couple and Todd in the swimming area when we arrived.

Todd came down from his post when he saw us coming. "Hey, Kincaid. Hey, Joe. What's up?" All I could think about was that he'd taken Veronica's virginity over the weekend.

I kept walking toward the water's edge while Joseph spoke to him. "I'm going to help her learn to swim," he said.

"Let me know if you need any help," Todd said. He started to walk away and then came back. "Kincaid, could I talk to you for a minute?"

Joseph looked confused as I walked back to them. "What is it?" I asked.

"I just wanted to apologize for the other day when I tried to teach you to swim," he said. "I didn't mean to seem like I was laughing at you and didn't want you to get the wrong idea. Veronica had this idea you might have a little crush on me, but I told her that wasn't the case, because that's crazy, right? I mean, it does happen to me sometimes..."

Blood rushed to my cheeks as I looked down at my feet. "That's crazy," I said, desperately trying to maintain what was left of my dignity as I forced myself to face Todd. "Veronica doesn't have to worry about that because I don't have a crush on you."

He sighed with relief. "Good, because I'm practically an old man compared to you."

Todd was nowhere near an old man and still extremely attractive, but whatever crush I'd felt before was long gone in the presence of Joseph. Even more so when he took my hand in front of Todd—saving me from further embarrassment, and I loved him for it.

It was rather arrogant for Todd to assume I had a crush on him, although it was once true. He finally floated back down to Earth from the cloud of his ego and noticed Joseph's hand in mine. "Oh." Todd raised his eyebrows as he looked at Joseph and me. "So, you two are dating?" Were we officially dating? I had no idea.

Joseph glanced at me, and I hoped he didn't notice the panic in my face as he turned to Todd. "Yeah, we are," he said with a smile. *Well, that answered my question.* Joseph walked to the bank where I had dropped my towel, tugging me along with him.

"So...we're dating?" I was anxious to hear him say it again.

"Sorry about that," he said, looking at the ground and shuffling the sand with his bare feet. "I thought Todd was insulting you more than he was apologizing, and now, all I see is the guy who's sleeping with my sister. It irritates me that he's so full of himself sometimes."

"He does have a pretty big ego, doesn't he?" I asked, glancing at the lifeguard stand in time to catch Todd looking at us. He waved and turned away.

"Told you so," Joseph said with a smirk, revealing a tiny dimple on his cheek. "He's not all bad, though. He can't be if Veronica loves him."

I thought my knees might buckle underneath me. "So, did you mean it about the dating thing?" I asked.

He looked out at the lake and dropped his towel on the ground beside mine. "Are you allowed to date?"

"I don't know." And I didn't; I'd asked my mom's permission to continue seeing him, but she didn't answer. The only mention of dating was when Mom told me I was too young for a boyfriend. "I guess so since my grandparents let me go out with you on Friday. Are you allowed?" My mouth was beginning to taste like feet as many times as I'd stuck my foot in it. I covered my mouth with my hand. "Shit. I'm sorry. I didn't mean..."

Joseph moved my hand away from my mouth. "Kincaid, it's okay," he said. "Veronica's my guardian until I turn eighteen, and considering she's sleeping with the lifeguard, I don't think she'll mind me dating you. If you want that..."

My mouth went completely numb and dry. "I do want that," I choked. He stepped forward and full-body hugged me, and I could have died right there.

"Come on, let's swim," he said, dragging me by both hands toward the water.

My body was already floating, and my head was swimming.

Chapter 17

J oseph was a better teacher than Todd because he made the water more fun. By the first week of July, he had me swimming five, ten, fifteen, and finally twenty feet into his waiting arms, once I finally got the hang of floating on my stomach. We laughed together the whole time.

One afternoon, after I'd had my fill of swimming, we went for a walk down to the old dock where I'd go to sit with Eduardo every evening.

"I think I like this dock the best," I said as I sat down and let my feet dangle in the water. "It's my new favorite writing place." I told Joseph about my conversations with Eduardo and a little about my writing.

"I have to read four books this summer, and write some reports and comparisons," he said as he sat beside me. "I had to take an incomplete in English."

"What books?"

"*A Separate Peace, The Scarlet Letter, The Hot Zone,* and *To Kill a Mockingbird.*"

"Have you started any of them? I've read them all."

"Heather said I should read *The Scarlet Letter* first to get it over with. And she was right; I don't really care for it much. I'm about halfway through it."

"What do you not like about it?" I wondered if he had a problem reading about adultery. I thought the story was interesting but had to admit I wasn't a fan of the long-winded writing style.

"It's just...dry and wordy, I guess. I feel exhausted after reading a couple of pages."

I laughed. "I thought the same thing. Don't worry, the others are better. *A Separate Peace* is probably my favorite, and *To Kill a Mockingbird* made me cry, but I loved it. *The Hot Zone* freaked me out because it's about a virus outbreak."

"I think I'll read *The Hot Zone* next since it sounds more exciting than Puritan adultery. What did you like best about the others?"

I told him all I could without revealing too much of the plot or the endings. He listened and smiled while I talked, occasionally moving a strand of hair behind my ear so it wouldn't tickle his face since we were sitting so close.

"I can't wait to discuss the books with you as I read them."

"This subject isn't torture for you?"

"Nah," he said. "I actually like to read, and I really like talking to you, especially when you're talking about books. Your whole face lights up." I could feel it turning red as he brushed my cheek with his fingers, bumping my glasses. "Your eyes..."

"What about them?"

"When you're excited about something, there's this navy ring around the green that's more noticeable." He was close enough to kiss me if either of us had moved forward, but I was afraid to move.

"Your eyes have some green in them too," I said. I was all trashed out with lake hair, but I didn't care at the moment. *Please, God, let him kiss me,* I thought. But he didn't.

"Yeah," he said, suppressing a grin.

Movement behind Joseph caught my attention. I looked over his shoulder and saw Grandpa walking toward us. "Hey, kids!" he called.

The volume of Grandpa's voice caused us both to jump, and I instantly felt guilty, even though I knew we weren't doing anything wrong.

"Hey, Mr. Kincaid," Joseph said, standing up. He held out his hand to help me.

"Thought you'd want to go with me to pick out fireworks for the show."

"Is Grandma going too?" I asked, taking Joseph's hand to stand. Our fingers lingered together before I took a step sideways as gracefully as I could while stumbling over my own flip-flops.

Grandpa shook his head and chuckled. "They're running one of them *Matlock* marathons on the TV. She wants to stay here to watch her program, and she's always let me pick them out before. I think she trusts me with all the explosive things."

"That's a lot of trust for a man who enjoys fire so much," Joseph said, sharing an inside joke with my grandfather. It was strange and sweet that they had a relationship with each other I knew so little about.

"Ed might like to go with us. I'll go ask him." Grandpa disappeared on the trail leading back to the motel.

Joseph turned to me. "He's such a big kid about the Fourth. Last year, he had someone come out and set off a firework show on the other side of the lake. He said it wasn't as good as what he could do himself, so this year, he's wanting me to help him set off the blasts."

His lips still looked kissable, but the moment was long past. "That sounds fun."

Lesson 19: Kisses don't always happen when you expect them, especially when you're interrupted.

Soon we were off to the fireworks stand, Grandpa leading the way in his small truck. Joseph and I followed them, and I could see Ed's hands moving in every direction as he talked to Grandpa from the passenger seat.

"What do you think they're talking about up there?" I asked.

"The good old days, probably. They've told me a couple of their war stories. None of the heavy stuff, but some of their stories about traveling and the mess halls."

"Todd said it was pretty bad where he was stationed. He didn't go into a lot of detail but talked about a man who died and left behind his wife and baby girl. I don't see the point of it all—all the fighting. I wish countries could just work everything out by talking."

"Fighting for freedom," Joseph said. "At least that's what Ed said. It's been that way since the beginning of time. Hence the holiday we're about to celebrate."

But were they really fighting for freedom? I vaguely recalled watching war footage in my middle school when Todd must have been overseas fighting in 1991. It all seemed so far away—like it could never happen here in the United States. Then there were scary things closer to home. All those people who died in Waco, Texas, in '93. Then the Oklahoma City bombing just a couple of months ago in my own hometown. My father had referred to the incidents as senseless tragedies since so many innocent people had died. Children had died. But who got to decide who was innocent and who wasn't?

Innocent people died all the time. My brother died of cancer, a kid I went to elementary school with drowned, and Joseph's parents died in a car accident. All were innocent people who'd died tragically.

The events in Texas and Oklahoma had frightened me the most because it showed that bad things could happen anywhere—somewhere close to me. I was sure Joseph agreed considering his tragic circumstances.

Because I had been so lost in my thoughts, I didn't realize we'd reached our destination until Joseph's door slammed. I shook my head as he came around to my side to let me out.

"You okay?" he asked. I nodded, but I wasn't. "You don't look okay."

"We're celebrating a holiday for the ending of a war where innocent people died, Joseph. I've never really thought about it like that before." I hung my head and stared at our feet, which were almost touching, just like our lips had almost touched before. There were people all around us, judging by the noise; I wanted them all to disappear. Then, despite all the people around, Joseph kissed me...on my forehead. If he didn't kiss me for real soon, I thought I might go crazy.

"Let's go supervise your grandpa before he buys the whole supply." Joseph took my hand and pulled me away from my thoughts again. "And besides, think of it as celebrating my sixteenth birthday instead of celebrating the end to a war."

"Your birthday's July 4? Why didn't you tell me sooner?"

He shrugged. "For years, I thought the fireworks were just for me."

"They can be this year, if you want."

Joseph's only response was to squeeze my hand.

After buying enough firework boxes to fill the backs of his and Joseph's trucks, Grandpa seemed satisfied with the show he'd be able to put on. During the shopping, I'd learned the fireworks at the lake were more than just a show for the motel guests. Several businesses in the area did their own shows on the lake and entertained town residents and guests for miles along the bank. Grandpa said he couldn't confirm nor deny the existence of a friendly wager between some of the businesses over whose display would be the biggest and loudest. Ed seemed thrilled to be part of the action, so Joseph dutifully bowed out to allow them their glory.

I was glad Joseph would be a spectator for other reasons. Mainly that our kiss had been interrupted. If he had planned to kiss me. Was I reading too much into the whole situation? The forehead kiss had felt way more intimate than the kiss on the cheek he'd given me after our date. Maybe each kiss would progress until he reached my lips. I needed to call Courtney.

"Oh my gosh, yes!" Courtney squealed after I'd told her about the developments between Joseph and me. "Kissing on the forehead while he's hugging you is much more meaningful than an awkward peck on the lips! How can you be almost sixteen and not know this? The forehead kiss means he really, really cares about you! Don't you ever watch movies? Lord knows, you read enough books that there should have been a romance novel or two in the mix by now."

"You're still coming for the Fourth of July celebration, right? I want you to meet Joseph."

"As long as my step-monster doesn't change my dad's mind."

"You said she's not that bad."

"Just wait and see when you have one. It comes and goes sometimes."

I didn't need to be reminded of my parents' marital issues. My feelings for Joseph distracted me in the best way possible, but my dreams still drifted into reality as I slept each night. I hated to admit I was rooting more for their split-up than against it lately.

"Shit, Kincaid, I didn't mean it. I'm sorry."

"Talk to you when you get here, Court." I heard her start to say something else, but I hung up the phone anyway.

Who did she think she was? The expert on divorce since her parents had gone through it? My parents weren't the same as hers. Or were they? Maybe they were like some of my other friends' parents. Did Dad already have a new girlfriend? I knew my mom wouldn't have had time to see anyone since she was always working or wanting me to talk to her. One of my friends was still pretty mad at her mother three years later for having an affair that had ended her parents' marriage.

I couldn't imagine Dad doing that to Mom, or to me, even if he couldn't seem to look at me lately. Maybe he didn't believe me that Derek was a one-time mistake. I probably wouldn't see him much if Mom moved us here. At least I would have Joseph to help me get through it.

Who would I be here? Would I really fit in with Joseph's friends? They were all so accepting and perfect. How long would it be before I messed up again or wasn't good enough for them? But what if I could be good like Joseph? I could go to church with him and sign the purity pledge too. There'd be no pressure from him and lots of kissing to make my heart flutter like a dandelion seed floating in the wind.

I could start over here and not be labeled as a troublemaker or a naïve girl desperately chasing a bad boy. Besides Courtney, who was I really leaving behind at my school? There were several kids I hung out with during school events with Courtney, but would any of them really miss me if I moved away? Courtney and I could still keep in touch and talk on the phone every night. She wouldn't forget about me. Would she?

The morning of the Fourth, I woke up to the phone ringing in my room. I glanced at the clock radio as I grabbed the phone from the nightstand. It wasn't even seven o'clock yet. "Hello," I mumbled.

"Did I wake you?" my mother asked, cheerier than I'd heard her in months.

"Yeah, but it's fine. My alarm would've gone off in an hour anyway. What's up?"

"Nothing, I just wanted to wish you a happy Fourth and remind you to be careful around the fireworks. My friend in high school lost her eyesight in one eye after being hit with a spark."

"I know, Mom," I groaned. "I promise I won't touch them. Grandpa and his friend are going to set everything off above the lake, and I'll hang back with Courtney, Joseph, and his friends—my friends now, too."

"I'm sorry Dad and I can't be there with you." She seemed like she had more to say but kept silent. All I heard was a clicking sound on the line.

"Mom?"

"Yeah, sweetheart?"

"Just making sure you were still there." I twisted the phone cord around my fingers. I hated having to apologize to my mom because it meant I had hurt her, but at least it was easier to do without having to look into her eyes. "I'm sorry. Really sorry for disappointing you and Dad."

"Kincaid..." *Great, more silence.* She sighed and coughed a bit. "Honey, we both love you so much. We just want you to be happy and stay out of trouble. Trouble has a way of stealing your future, and we don't want to see anything bad happen to you, ever. If I could prevent all pain from your whole life just by taking it on myself, I would, baby."

I couldn't stop myself from crying after hearing that. "Mom, if you and Dad get divorced and you move here, I want to stay with you. Please let me do that."

"Oh, Kincaid, sweetheart, nothing's been decided yet. We're trying really hard to work things out so that doesn't happen."

"Even if it doesn't happen, moving here might help...to get out of that house." I grabbed a tissue from the box on the nightstand and wiped my face and nose.

"I know, baby, I know. We've talked about that too. I'm going to let you go so you can get some more rest. Just be safe tonight and have fun with your friends. Mom told me a lot about Joseph, and I'm glad you've made a new friend."

"He's more than that, Mom. I think...I don't know exactly what we are yet."

"It's okay to not know, Kincaid. It's the best part of living—the excitement of figuring it all out. Goodbye, sweetheart. I love you so much."

"I love you too, Mom." I hung up the phone, got up, and cried my remaining tears in the shower. Since I was already up, I crept into my grandparents' apartment and was met with the aroma of bacon I'd grown accustomed to.

"Well, look who's up with the chickens," Grandpa said with a chuckle. "Didn't expect to see you up so early on a holiday."

"We still have some guests checking in later today, Grandpa. I want to make sure my best friend's room is perfect for her."

"Ah, that's right," Grandma said. "Courtney's mom confirmed the reservations yesterday. They'll check in around one o'clock today, in time for the evening cookout and festivities."

"Stepmom," I corrected.

"Well, that don't make a lick of difference," Grandpa said. "I'm anxious to meet this best friend of yours. Joseph's been giving her some real competition so far, so I hope she's prepared for it."

Grandma laughed and kissed Grandpa on the cheeks. "In all your years, you've still learned nothing about women," she laughed. "Girlfriends tell each other everything, especially about boys."

I nodded in agreement with Grandma as I helped myself to some bacon and the most mouthwatering silver-dollar pancakes I'd ever eaten. They seemed to get better each time Grandma made them for me.

As soon as breakfast was cleared away and I'd rushed through my morning chores, I ran back to my grandma's kitchen to make a special birthday cake for Joseph. Grandma would never dream of letting me use a boxed mix, so she supervised me while I used her favorite recipe, which came from a Home Economics textbook from the 1930s. The fudge icing recipe came straight from the side of the can of Hershey's Cocoa and was surprisingly more difficult to make than the cake because of having to measure out the shortening.

"They say a way to a man's heart is through his stomach," Grandma said as I spread the last of the frosting across the cake. The layers were a bit uneven, but I didn't think Joseph would mind too much. "I suppose that's true for a teenage boy too."

"It's just a birthday cake, Grandma, not a marriage proposal."

"I hope I live to see you get married, Kincaid."

"Geez, Grams, way to be morbid. Of course, you'll live to see me get married someday."

She sat down on her stool. "I'll either be there in person or in spirit, my dear child…in person or in spirit."

I hated when she spoke like that. I never wanted to think about her not being around anymore. I smiled at her as I put the glass cover over Joseph's cake. "Not bad for my first cake. I couldn't have done it without your help, Grandma. I would never have thought to sift the powdered sugar for the icing."

She grinned. "It keeps the lumps out."

I carefully placed the cake in the refrigerator and began cleaning up my mess. I wanted to hide all the evidence before Joseph dropped by to get Grandma's list for the grocery store.

Later, when Courtney arrived, we spent the first few seconds jumping and squealing as we hugged each other. I couldn't believe how different she looked when I saw her. Her dark brown hair, which had been past her waist when school ended, was now cut to her chin in the cutest bob I'd ever seen. It made her look so much older than me, even though I was still several inches taller than her.

Her little sister, Mauve, who looked nothing like her with bright red hair and freckles, cowered behind their dad until I called her over, "Come here, squirt," I said, motioning for her to join us in our hug. "I've missed you, too, and can't wait to hear about how big your new pony is now." Mauve giggled as I picked her up and spun her around until she was dizzy. Courtney rolled her eyes and shook her head. I didn't get her hostility with her sister sometimes. I would've gladly taken Mauve off her hands, considering that she idolized her big sister. Of course, there were other times when the two got along so well that no one would have ever guessed the sisters argued at all.

"Y'all will love the lake," I continued as Courtney's parents joined us. "I hope you brought your suits."

"They did," Courtney's stepmom, Marcy, said. "Unfortunately, though, we can only stay for one night, Kincaid. I have to go back to work on Thursday."

"Yeah, it sucks," Courtney mumbled. Her dad, Kent, glared at her as she spoke.

"Young lady," Kent said. "We drove several hours to get here. The phrase you're looking for is 'Thank you, Marcy, for rearranging your work schedule so I can be here with my best friend for the Fourth.'"

Courtney repeated his phrase and then walked back to their car to start unloading. I just grinned awkwardly at her parents until Marcy spoke to me. "Kincaid," she said, placing her hand on my shoulder. "Thank you so much for inviting us for the celebration. This place is beautiful."

"You staying out of trouble, kiddo?" Kent nudged my shoulder.

"Yes, sir, and you're welcome, Marcy," I said. Courtney's dad walked back to the car to help his daughters unload.

"I spoke with your mother a few days ago," Marcy continued, stepping closer to me so she could speak more softly. "Kincaid, for the record, I believed Courtney from the beginning when she said Derek was at fault for the whole fiasco. It took a little more convincing for Kent, but he came around once I explained to him how important a girl's best friend is to her development."

I never knew any of those things when Courtney had cried to me on the phone and told me her parents may not let her hang out with me anymore after I got home from being bailed out. I always assumed they had both been against me. Marcy's psychologist profession had come to my aid, and I owed her more than the hug I offered. She embraced me and excused herself to finish unloading their vehicle.

I took Courtney and Mauve to the lake while their parents napped. Todd was watching the other kids who were staying at the motel as they swam with their families. Courtney stopped on the trail and fanned herself with her hat. "Oh, my God, Kincaid," she whispered. "Is that *the* Todd? He's so hot."

I laughed. "Down, girl. He's dating Joseph's sister, Veronica. And he's too old for you, anyway."

"I'm older than you."

"I don't think the three months of extra life you've had takes you off the jailbait list."

"What's jailbait?" Mauve asked, frowning at me. *Oops. I'd forgotten she was there for a moment.*

"It's what you call someone who's too young to date a grown-up," Courtney said.

I gasped. "Courtney!"

131

She turned to me. "What? She's got to learn sometime. Mauve and I have a rule—no lying to each other—right, squirt?" In a rare moment of public affection, Courtney put her arm around her sister, and Mauve grinned at me.

We hung out at the lake all afternoon discussing the rest of our summer plans and had a PG-rated discussion about my maybe-relationship with Joseph, which I was dying to have evolve into a kissing kind of relationship. At ten years old, Mauve still giggled at the talk of kissing boys and said the whole thing sounded disgusting considering that some boys at her school still ate their boogers. We assured her that even booger-eaters could grow up to be cute teenagers who had brushed their teeth enough times throughout the years to remove any booger residue, but Mauve still looked skeptical.

Even with her general disgust of boys, Mauve was still on board with helping me surprise Joseph for his birthday. Courtney was ready to help distract him long enough for me to slip away from the festivities to get the cake. I'd already put in a call to Amy so she could call their friends about the surprise party.

Even the DJ who'd come by to do a sound and power check was in on the surprise and would be ready to play a special song at my signal later in the evening after the fireworks were finished. I was growing more excited about it by the minute.

Chapter 19

By evening, the entire lake area had been transformed into a festive barbeque wonderland. There were paper lanterns, torches, and repurposed white and red Christmas lights strung up everywhere to light the docks and picnic area. Red, white, and blue flags decorated every pole set up for that purpose. Several local businesses had hauled in large grills, smokers, and a food truck to feed everyone who'd gathered at the motel. Some people were guests, others I recognized from the church, and some I'd never seen before. Caution tape roped off the lake because no swimming would be allowed during the festivities—not that night swimming was allowed anyway.

The temperature was still in the nineties, but at least a mild breeze kept the heat manageable as darkness came. The heat might have been manageable, but the mosquitos were a different story. Even with the citronella torches and bug repellant I'd slathered on, there were still mosquitos buzzing around my face and tickling my ears.

Joseph got along well with Courtney, and I loved seeing him interact with Mauve. Amy, Dustin, Heather, and Kevin showed up, too, as we'd planned, and hung out with all of us. Mindy showed up with a group of other kids who seemed nice enough. At least she wasn't all over Joseph since he rarely left my side. And Joseph had no issue putting his arm around me in front of Mindy as we sipped our sodas and enjoyed our burgers and hot dogs. Being the owners' granddaughter certainly worked to my advantage when it was time for the fireworks because my friends and I were able to take over my favorite old dock to watch the show.

In between the displays, Grandpa and Ed's laughter echoed off the trees surrounding the lake. The party barge they occupied sat anchored in the center of the lake in the perfect spot to make the sky light up above the whole area.

"Where's Todd?" Courtney asked as she nudged me. "I might have to fall into the lake and let him save me."

I looked around to see if I could spot him in the crowd. Aunt Sylvia stood near some volunteer firefighters who were still cooking hot dogs near their truck. Todd was nowhere to be seen, and the other lifeguard was standing near the station even though the water was off-limits at night. It seemed weird that he and Veronica would be missing the show. Both knew about the surprise coming up for Joseph.

"Where's your sister?" I asked Joseph.

He looked around. "I'm not sure."

We all jumped as booms shook the dock. Grandpa and Ed were starting the finale, which was crazy loud in comparison to the mild sizzles of the other fireworks. In between the explosions, the crowd gasped and applauded. I held my fingers in my ears and watched in awe, leaned against Joseph. As the noise stopped, I unplugged my ears and heard panicked screaming coming from near the lifeguard tower. Male screaming.

"Make it stop!" the voice screeched.

The firefighters cleared a path in the crowd, and under the tower's lights, I could see a man drop to the ground and cover his head with his arms. Todd knelt beside him, but I couldn't hear what he was saying.

"The noise—he can't handle it," Joseph said. "That's Todd's friend who was in the hospital the same time as Veronica. Burn-unit stuff."

I'd read about post-traumatic stress, but I'd never known anyone who suffered from it. A news report I'd seen featured several people, most of them ex-military, who could be set off by sounds or even certain smells to make them believe they were back in the war. It was terrifying to watch the reenactments; I couldn't imagine having to watch someone I loved go through that. Poor Todd. He seemed so strong as he held his friend in a bear hug. He must have been strong for everyone in his unit, too, when they were overseas.

The firefighters jumped into action to help calm the man. The crowd backed up as I walked forward to where Aunt Sylvia was standing near the grills.

"Poor guy," Sylvia said as I reached her side.

Joseph came up behind me and put his hand on my shoulder as we watched Todd and one of the firefighters escort his friend into the back of a waiting ambulance. I caught a glimpse of the deep scarring on the man's arms and legs, a deep pink against his dark skin.

"Shrapnel from a bomb," Joseph said. "He's covered in scars from it. That's Adam; he saved the lives of several other men by pushing them out of the way. He suffered some third-degree burns on his chest and back too."

"A broken-hearted man," Sylvia said. "He still thinks about the men he couldn't save. I saw him when I visited Veronica at the hospital. He's only a couple of years older than her. Only eighteen when he enlisted. He helped out with Dane's peewee baseball team years ago. Such a good kid. Bless his heart."

"A hero," I said.

By the time the ambulance silently pulled away with its lights flashing, the energy of the crowd had dissipated. Grandpa and Ed were back on shore and filled in on what had happened. I could tell Grandpa felt guilty that his loud fireworks had set off Adam, but it was nothing that could have been prevented. One of the firefighters told him he'd seen a veteran set off by a backfiring car once.

Lesson 20: Veterans have to deal with more than most people understand.

I was still shaken by the whole experience when I slipped away to get Joseph's cake. Veronica had followed the ambulance to the hospital to be with Todd and his friend, but I didn't want to ignore Joseph's birthday—his first one without his parents. I watched him as I cautiously made my way back to the picnic table where he sat with Courtney and his friends. The look on Joseph's face when I arrived with the cake topped with sparklers was enough proof I'd made the right decision. His eyes watered as they met mine while the entire crowd sang along with the DJ to wish him a happy birthday.

Chapter 20

After Courtney and her family left, hotel business picked up for the next week. When I wasn't working with Sylvia and Veronica or hanging out with Joseph, I spent my time absorbing every detail Ed was willing to share with me. He'd enjoyed himself so much during the holiday that he decided to stay a while longer.

While Ed and Grandpa played chess in the afternoons, I would sit with them and listen to them reminisce about the good old days. Sometimes, while talking about Rosa, Ed would stop and stare at the board as if he were contemplating his next move. Grandpa seemed to know the pain in his friend's soul and waited as long as it took for Ed to regain his composure and make a move. None of the moves made much sense to me, even when Ed tried to describe the game as telling a story.

One evening, Ed joined me on the dock close to sunset. "Mind if I join you?" he asked, setting up his folding chair.

"Not at all," I said, pulling my knees up to my chest. "I think this is my favorite spot on the whole lake."

"Mine too."

We sat in silence for several minutes, enjoying the company of each other during our solitary thoughts. Ed had taught me to think like a writer, even though he claimed he just taught me how to listen to the voice that was already there. He seemed more tired than he had earlier in the summer, breathing more heavily.

"Are you doing okay, Ed? Is it too hot out here for you?"

"Nah," he gasped. "It's just the damn humidity. Wet heat feels hotter than the dry heat I'm used to. And maybe I'm getting a summer cold or something." He took a handkerchief from his pocket and wiped his brow.

"Thank you for spending so much time with me talking about writing, sir. I'll never forget this as long as I live."

"The honor is mine. I expect great writing from you as you grow, Kincaid. I'll be just a sidebar in your story. But those grandparents of yours, they'll hold a far bigger place if you'll take every bit of life they're willing to share with you."

"I'll make sure to write about all of it. Did Grandpa tell you about the challenge he gave me when I showed up here?"

Ed chuckled. "He sure did." He took a drink from his thermos and got strangled a bit. "Don't tell your cousins, but you're your grandpa's favorite. He told me so."

I felt myself blushing, not sure I deserved "favorite" status from anyone.

Ed kept talking in short bursts. "Chester thinks you hung the moon, Kincaid. I remember him calling me after you were born, so proud of his youngest grandchild and the fact that you'd have his name."

"I used to think it was a stupid name."

"Don't ever think that. Imagine how good it will look on a book cover someday. Kincaid Walsh. It has a nice ring to it."

"Maybe you're right."

"I'm often right these days—one of the benefits of bein' older than dirt. Now, I'm leaving this place tomorrow, so make sure to practice your writing when I'm gone."

"I promise."

I helped Ed carry his things back to his room and left him for the evening.

As soon as I got back to my room, I wrote down another lesson from Ed.

Lesson 21: Practice your talent as often as possible.

I fell asleep while using the back of my notebook to write down every single sensation I felt when I spent time with Joseph. If I was, in fact, falling in love, I wanted every moment of it documented.

The next morning, Joseph showed up on his day off to work on my diving skills, which were lacking. After several failed attempts for a graceful entrance into the water, I gave up and pulled Joseph off the dock with me. Through all the splashing and laughing, I could barely hear my Grandpa when he walked out onto the dock and called to us. Joseph hopped out of the water first and helped me back up.

"Have either of you seen Ed? He told me last night he might go for a walk by the lake today," Grandpa said. "I thought I'd see if he was here since he didn't answer his door. I wanted to invite him to lunch before he leaves. You're welcome to come too, Joe, if you don't have other plans."

Joseph nodded as he dried off.

"I haven't seen him today, Grandpa," I said, looking around for Ed or his folding chair as I wrapped my towel around me to cover my swimsuit. "We chatted here on the dock yesterday evening. Could he have left early?"

Grandpa shook his head. "His car's still in the lot, and he'd never leave without saying goodbye to me."

"I haven't seen him either," Joseph said. "Maybe he went to the walking trail."

"I didn't think about that," Grandpa said. "I'm going to check the playground again before I go back to my place. Will you kids walk the trail and see if he's out there?"

Joseph slipped on his flip-flops and looked at me. "Sure."

We scoured the trail and saw several of the other guests, but no Ed. "I wonder where he went?" I asked. "Was Ed's car in the parking lot when you got here?"

"I don't know," Joseph said as he stopped and leaned against a tree. "But I wasn't really paying attention."

"Let's go back and check his room. Grandpa probably just missed him. He might have been in the shower or something."

I knocked on the door to Ed's room and listened for movement inside. It was eerily quiet all around us. No birds chirping. No cars on the highway. No kids playing on the playground. Just the hollow sound of my knocking.

Joseph peered in through the tiny crack in the curtain and looked back at me. "I think he's sitting in the chair asleep. I can see the lamp on."

My skin grew clammy after I tried to open the door and found it locked. "Do you have a key?" I asked, glancing at the *Do Not Disturb* sign hanging on the doorknob. Something wasn't right; I could feel it.

"Sylvia does."

"Keep knocking. I'll be right back." I ran past the rooms until I reached an open door and the cleaning cart. Veronica and Sylvia were laughing as they made the bed.

"Hey, Kincaid," Sylvia said. "Looks like you've been swimming."

"I need your keys."

"Oh," she said, handing them to me. "You lock yourself out?"

"No," I said as I ran from the room.

"Kincaid!" she called.

I arrived at Ed's room, where Joseph was still knocking and calling out for him. Sylvia and Veronica were on my heels by the time I reached the door.

"Kincaid, you can't just open a guest's door," Sylvia said, trying to get the keys back from me. "Especially when they have the sign on the door."

"I think something's wrong," I said, my voice shaking. I handed the keys to Joseph. "Just open it."

Joseph unlocked the door, but the chain was in place. He pressed his head in the crack and looked inside the room. I squatted below him to do the same. Ed was sitting in the chair by the lamp with a book in his lap, and his head was tilted back like he was asleep. For a moment, I was relieved, but then I noticed the unnatural angle of his neck. I turned to Sylvia and could feel my lip quivering. Ed was gone.

"Oh, dear God," she said. "Move." She pushed Joseph and me out of the way so she could look. "Joe, go get some bolt cutters, quick! And Veronica, call for help, now! Kincaid, go get your Grandpa."

We all ran to fulfill our assignments. It was hard to run in flip-flops, but I made it to my grandparents' apartment quickly. I didn't realize I was crying when I burst through their door until they jumped up at the sight of me.

"Kincaid!" Grandma said, rushing over to me. "What's wrong?"

I could hardly speak. "It's Ed, he's…"

Grandpa clamped his hand over his mouth and hurried outside without uttering a word. Grandma and I followed him.

Sylvia and Joseph were already in Ed's room when I stumbled back there. I could barely see through my tears as I crossed the room's threshold and looked at Ed sitting dead in the chair. Sylvia was kneeling beside him, checking for a pulse on his wrist. She tried both, then rose and checked his neck. Grandpa sat on the bed watching her, his forehead wrinkled and his knees shaking. Joseph stood near the window looking helpless, the bolt cutters still in his hand.

Grandma came up behind me and put her hand on my shoulder, giving it a squeeze. There was no use trying to resuscitate him, for Grandpa determined it had been too long as he looked down at his friend. We all stood in a silent vigil for Ed while we waited for help to arrive.

Veronica came back to the doorway at the same time we heard vehicles in the distance getting closer. An ambulance and a police car pulled into the parking lot as Joseph, Veronica, and I left the room. Joseph mumbled a greeting to the officers as he walked by. The three of us stood back and watched as everything buzzed around us.

Sylvia gave a statement to the police officer, which Joseph and I confirmed. A few minutes later, the coroner's vehicle arrived. I watched my grandfather stoically follow behind his friend's body on a stretcher until it was loaded up and driven away. Afterward, he and Grandma headed toward the walking trail, holding hands as they walked.

Before they left, an officer sealed the room with tape and instructed us not to go inside until they could complete their investigation with the state police over the next few days. By that time, a few other guests had gathered on the sidewalk to see what was going on. Sylvia informed them an elderly man had died peacefully in his sleep and offered to restock the mini-fridges free-of-charge. The guests declined and returned to their rooms or went on to their vehicles to leave the motel property, doing their best to live their lives as though nothing had happened.

"Has this ever happened before?" Veronica asked Sylvia.

"Unfortunately, yes," she said. "We had a man die from a heart attack on the walking trail a few years ago, and there was another death in one of the rooms when I worked here as a teenager."

"Which room?" Veronica asked. "What happened?"

Sylvia looked at Joseph and me before she answered. "A young woman committed suicide. Pills." She sighed. "I found her. I was sixteen, and it was the most terrible thing I'd ever seen. It was the same room Mr. Martinez died in."

Cold sweat formed all over my body, and I just had to get away from the room—convinced it was cursed. I walked back to my room and sat on the bench outside the door. There would be no more Eduardo Martinez poetry—his voice silenced—such a profound loss I couldn't grasp how much pain I felt from it. Was I even allowed to feel so much for a man I barely knew?

Lesson 22: All people deserve to have someone cry for them when they die.

I had to keep moving. I got up and followed the trail to the lake and tried to make myself disappear into the trees when I noticed a family with three kids playing near the water. They didn't need to see me cry. And I sure as hell didn't want Todd to see me cry, but his eyes were focused on the kids splashing in the shallow water despite their parents chasing after them. I leaned against a pine tree and looked at one of the docks. Just yesterday, Ed had sat there in his little chair, so full of life as he gave me writing advice. Now he was gone, and no one else in the world knew but us.

Dropping my head into my hands, I cried harder than I ever had, no longer caring who saw me. When arms wrapped around me, I fell into them and knew by the scent they belonged to Joseph. He held me close to his chest until my sobs dissolved into snuffs and hiccups. I wanted to run and hide from him to escape the embarrassment of falling apart, but at the same time, I never wanted him to let me go.

I raised my head to look at him again. Through my tear-soaked glasses, his warm brown eyes were somber. He pushed my hair behind my ears and dried the remaining tears off my cheeks with his thumbs.

"It's going to be okay," Joseph said. "He's in a better place now."

"I know, but I'm just so sad he died alone."

"Kincaid, he's with Rosa."

He was right, and that's all it took to comfort me because I no longer felt like crying.

Joseph's hands were still on my face when he kissed my forehead, and I closed my eyes and wrapped my arms around his neck. As I felt him pull away slightly, I opened my eyes. Then, before I could process what was happening, we both moved toward each other again. I'm sure I looked a mess with puffy eyes and air-dried, messy lake hair but that's when it happened for me—my first real kiss.

I felt his lips brush against mine, soft and sweet. I closed my eyes again as he captured my top lip with just enough pressure to make me understand how to kiss him back, and it was over as quickly as it began. He hugged me again, and I felt different afterward; I felt connected to him on a new level.

Lesson 23: A kiss that happens when you least expect it can change everything.

Chapter 21

Watching my grandfather mourn his friend was like nothing I'd ever seen before. He smiled at me and hugged me like always the next morning, but his eyes weren't smiling. It seemed like the bottom and top halves of his face were disconnected, severed by the pain in his heart. I still felt a dull ache from the loss of Ed, but my tears were already spent on that subject, stopped somehow by Joseph's kiss.

After a silent breakfast with my grandparents, I grabbed my notebook and wandered down to the dock where Ed and I had sat. It was the place where I wished for Joseph to kiss me. The sun hadn't been up very long, and I wanted to bask in the sounds of the lake and the birds that surrounded it. I watched them as they flew across the sky, seeming to freefall in movements like what Joseph had shown me in the water. The birds were sky-swimmers, floating just below where I believed heaven to be—where I hoped Ed was reunited with Rosa.

Ed was a traveler just visiting long enough to leave a legacy of love through his poetry. I wanted that too—a legacy of more than just getting arrested at fifteen for making a stupid mistake. I wasn't going to get in trouble again. I was going to improve my science grade in school (wherever that may be) in the fall. I was going to do everything I could to forgive my parents for lying to me and falling out of love if that was the case. I wasn't going to be a teenage pregnancy statistic. I was going to keep writing poetry. I would do all those things because Ed had believed in me even though we only spent a few brief moments together. It had to mean something.

And Joseph was much more complex than I could have imagined when I first met him. There was so much pain locked inside of him that the thought of it breaking out frightened me, not for myself, but for him. I wanted to be there for him and share the burden of it so he wouldn't have to feel it all by himself—a connection that felt deeper than any friendship I'd had in my entire life.

I heard him approaching long before his feet hit the dock, but I didn't turn around. I waited for Joseph to come to me. Soon, he was at my side on the dock, taking in the sights and sounds. "Are you okay?" he asked as he reached for my hand.

I nodded and squeezed his hand. "I was thinking about Ed. I'm sad, but I'm okay."

"He seemed like a good man. I've read some of his poetry in school." He leaned back to reach for something laying behind him on the dock.

"What's this?" I asked as he handed me a rolled-up piece of paper tied with a piece of twine.

"Open it."

It was a sketch of the dock with Ed and me sitting on it, everything detailed down to the wooden planks, my messy hair, and Ed's folding chair. "Oh, wow," I said. "This is…gosh, I don't know what to say."

"I finished the shading when I got home last night. I started it the day before yesterday. I saw you and Ed out here when I came back to pick up something for Veronica. I didn't want to disturb you, so I did the basic sketch and worked from a Polaroid I took. I hope you don't mind."

"No, I don't mind. This is beautiful. I had no idea you were an artist until Ed told me."

"Ah, he told you? You didn't say anything. It's just a hobby, really."

"I suppose he told you I shared a poem with him?" I looked at Joseph and raised my eyebrows.

Joseph ran his fingers through his hair. "He might have said something about a poem. Do I get to read it?"

"Do you really want to?"

"I showed you mine, now show me yours." Joseph blushed as soon as my mouth dropped open. "That's not what I meant…"

I laughed and handed him the notebook. He smiled and bit his lip a couple of times while he read my poem. I had never been so invested in watching someone else read my work. His opinion of it mattered to me more than anyone else's would. He pressed his lips together in a tight line as he handed the notebook back to me. I watched him, silently wishing for him to say something…anything.

"Thanks for sharing this with me, Kincaid," he said. "I think you're a great writer."

"Thanks for yesterday."

"The swimming lessons?"

"For everything. For letting me fall apart on you and to help me stop…you kissed me."

"I did. I hope it wasn't out of line."

"No. I thought you were going to kiss me while we were here on the dock before Grandpa came out. I wanted to kiss you then."

He laughed. "Yeah, I wanted to then too."

"I just can't believe my first kiss was when my face was all snotty. You do remember that it was my first kiss, right?"

He nodded and took my hand. "I remembered."

"So, how many girls have you kissed?"

"Three," he said with a smirk.

"Wow," I said, my hand over my heart. "Scandalous."

"The first two were silly spin-the-bottle kisses that didn't mean anything. Only the last one was on purpose. It actually meant something to me."

"So, four, including me. What happened to the one that mattered? Did she break your heart, or did you break hers?"

"I don't know yet."

What he said didn't make any sense. "Huh? How can you not know?"

He put his arm around my shoulders. "It's three including you. But as far as I'm concerned, you're the only one that counted. But since you don't think your appearance was perfect enough for a first kiss, I think you deserve a do-over."

I tried to appear calm on the outside. He was basically telling me I was his first real kiss, too, and he wanted to kiss me again. "Really?" I whispered, moving closer. He nodded and closed the distance to kiss me again. It lasted at least a full ten seconds with me screaming on the inside the whole time until someone clearing their throat interrupted us. We both jumped back and found Veronica standing behind us.

"Sorry to interrupt, but we've got work to do," she said. "Kincaid, can you help Sylvia and me for a little while?"

Joseph stood and helped me up. "I should probably get the mowing done before it gets too hot, anyway. See you later, Kincaid." He walked away and left me awkwardly standing there with his grinning sister.

"I didn't realize you and Joe had gotten to that level yet," she said. "I think it's sweet."

"I like him a lot," I told her as we walked back toward the motel.

Later, while we were remaking a bed in one of the rooms, Veronica started talking to me more seriously. "My brother is much stronger than I am. I would have given up if I didn't have him to live for. And then I met Todd, and everything seemed to get a little better for me. Todd doesn't know, but I was already falling in love with him long before we started dating. He's different when it's just us—a lot more sensitive than he acts around everyone else."

"I can see that."

"I'm going to marry him."

I chuckled. "What does Todd think about that?"

"It was his idea. He wants to reenlist after college. We'd need to be married so I would be taken care of if something were to happen to him."

"Shouldn't it be more about love than practicality? What about your college? And what about Joseph? You'd really want to pull him out of school? A year from now would be right before his senior year."

"Joseph would be fine anywhere, I think. He could go with us or stay here with one of his friends until he graduates."

I stopped walking and glared at her. "After everything, you'd just tear him out of school or leave him behind?"

She stopped walking too. "It's not that simple, Kincaid."

"You should talk to him before you make a decision that will affect him."

"Obviously. My brother and I have a good relationship."

"Then you know how much he needs his friends."

"And he knows how much I need to leave this place," she said with tears in her eyes. "I don't know how much longer I can stand the memories. The whole thing's my fault, and I have to live with it every day." She was crying harder, looking at the ground. "I was arguing with my parents the night this happened." She held out her arm in front of me, and I looked down at the scar on her arm, which stood out against her suntanned skin. "I just started remembering bits and pieces of that night— dreaming about them mostly. I don't know how to tell my brother."

Hearing Veronica blame herself would crush Joseph. After seeing him cry about how he felt after they died, I didn't think he could take it. "Don't. You should never tell him."

"But it's all my fault. He should know that."

"It's not your fault. Don't say stupid shit like that." She flinched as I ran my fingers over her scar. "I'm so sorry. I just really care about Joseph and don't want him hurt either."

Lesson 24: Not all scars are visible.

After an exhausting morning of vacuuming the vacant rooms, I took a break to eat lunch with my grandparents. Grandpa was distant and sad as he chewed his tuna sandwich. Grandma tried to keep the conversation going but ended up only talking to me after Grandpa responded in only grunts and nods.

"Are you and Joe going out on a date tonight, Kincaid?" she asked.

"I don't really know if I can call it dating, Grandma. Mom says I'm too young for a boyfriend."

"Don't you worry your pretty little head. I talked to Susan on the phone and convinced her that Joe's a good influence on you, friend or boyfriend."

Dating-life intervention from my grandma. I supposed stranger things had happened, just not to me. "Thanks, Grandma. I appreciate you fighting for me."

She shushed me and looked around the room. "Not just for you," she said. "For Joe. It's been so long since I've seen that poor boy smile. I think you're good for him too. He's suffered so much in his young life but has handled it with more class than men I've known three times his age."

A knock from the living room startled me, and Grandpa got up silently and shuffled to the door.

Joseph followed Grandpa back into the kitchen. "Good afternoon, Mrs. Kincaid," he said. "I came to ask permission to take Kincaid out again tonight." He turned to me. "If you're feeling up to it."

I wanted to feel up for going out, but with Ed's death so recent, I didn't. I felt so conflicted as I looked up at Joseph. He caught on right away. "I figured you wouldn't want to be around a big crowd," he continued. "So, I thought you might want to go with me to Amy's house to watch a movie. It'll just be her and Dustin. Heather and Kevin have rehearsals for ballet class."

Grandpa finally seemed to have life in him as he looked at me and then Joseph. "Will Amy's parents be home?" he asked gruffly. It was the most he'd spoken in the last hour. I hadn't even known he was paying attention to anything we said.

"Of course, sir," Joseph said. "Their number's in the church directory under 'Reynolds' if you want to call and confirm."

"Won't be necessary, son," Grandpa said. "You continue to be honest with me as you always have and treat Kincaid with the respect she deserves, and you and me will have no problems."

"Well, that settles it," Grandma said, turning to me. "Do you want to go? It might help take your mind off things."

"I'd love to go," I said. "But, please, no sad movies."

"Oh no," Joseph said. "Dustin's picking it, and he hates sad movies. He likes B-movies and is showing us the worst movie ever made tonight. He said it's great for a laugh. Something about trolls. If he says it's bad, then it must be considering some of the choices he's made lately."

I couldn't help but giggle. "Fine, I'll go since you're all twisting my arm."

"Home by ten o'clock," Grandpa said as I left the apartment.

"And have a good time!" Grandma called.

Out on the porch, Joseph took my hands. "I've got some things to take care of this afternoon, so I'll come back to get you around five, okay?"

"That's fine. I need a nap."

He gave me a quick peck on the lips and walked away, the sunlight creating a halo over his head as he approached the truck. He waved at me and drove away. I noticed Sylvia watching me from the sidewalk in front of one of the rooms. I walked down to where she stood.

"Hey, girl," she said. "How you holdin' up? You were pretty upset last night."

I followed her into the empty room, sat in one of the armchairs and watched her while she dusted. "I'll be all right. I'd never seen a dead person before. It was..." *Revolting, disgusting, sad, terrifying.*

She walked over and squeezed my shoulder. "I know, sweetheart," she said. "It wasn't easy for me either, and I've been through that before. I know you were getting pretty close with Ed, and it looks like you're getting pretty close with someone else we both know. Was that a kiss I just witnessed?"

My face grew warm. "Maybe," I smirked. "Grandma got involved, and my mom agreed to let me date him as long as we're not unsupervised."

"That's sweet," she said wistfully. "Young love."

"Love? Geez, let's start with strong like, Aunt Sylvia! Even Ed was jumping the gun assuming Joseph was already my boyfriend."

"Ed was a kindred spirit—a poet like you." She pulled something out of the pocket of her uniform and handed it to me. It was a small package, wrapped haphazardly in a cut-up paper grocery bag with my name scribbled on it in handwriting I instantly recognized—Ed's writing. "I found this in the nightstand drawer when the police collected Ed's personal belongings. It might not be right, but I told them this item was left behind by a previous guest and had not belonged to Ed because I wanted to make sure you got it. It must be special if he took the time to wrap it up for you."

I held the package in my hands, unsure of what to do with it. At Sylvia's urging, I tore open the corner and pulled out the little leather notebook Ed had shown me that contained his poem for Rosa. Tears filled my eyes as I held it to my chest. I had no idea why Ed had chosen to give me his prized notebook, but I vowed then to protect it and cherish it forever.

Lesson 25: The most thoughtful gifts contain a little piece of the giver's soul.

Chapter 22

A my lived in a nice older neighborhood past the mall. After meeting her parents, a hyper couple in their forties, Joseph and I went with Amy to the basement-level den where pizza, popcorn, and sodas were waiting.

"My brother's out with his girlfriend, so it's just us tonight. Dustin should be here soon with the movie."

As if on cue, Dustin trampled down the stairs and looked at the array of food and beverages. "What, no beer?"

Amy noticed my puzzled expression and giggled. "Relax, Kincaid. He's joking," she said. "Did you remember to get the movie, Dustin?"

"I got it!" he exclaimed. "The. Very. Last. Copy…of the worst movie ever made to date, *Troll 2*."

"One wasn't enough?" Joseph asked, resting his arm around my shoulders as we sat on the overstuffed couch.

"Despite popular misconception, the two movies are not related." Dustin opened the video case and pulled out the tape while laughing in a way that made him sound like the Count on *Sesame Street*.

"Is it scary?" Amy asked. She took the tape from him and placed it in her VCR. "Since, you've obviously seen it before."

"It's horrifyingly bad," Dustin said with a laugh. "But not what I'd call scary." He plopped down in a large bean bag with a slice of pizza while Amy dimmed the lights and grabbed her own food before she joined him on the bean bag, sitting on his lap.

Joseph got pizza for both of us and rejoined me on the couch as the movie started. We ate and watched the movie in absolute horror. Dustin wasn't kidding when he said it was the worst movie ever made. Just when I thought it couldn't get any worse, it did and exceeded my expectations each time. The best part of the whole experience was being sprawled out with Joseph, leaning against his chest. He had initiated holding me in front of his friends. I felt comfortable enough there to take my shoes off and pull my feet up on the couch.

Amy got up and turned the lights back up after the movie ended. She stood in front of Dustin, her arms crossed, tapping her foot. "What was that?" she asked. "I seriously want the last hour and a half of my life back."

Dustin burst into laughter. "I know!" he said, barely catching his breath. "Wasn't it awesome?"

Joseph started laughing, too, his chuckles shaking my whole body since I was still in his arms. "Oh. My. Gaaawwwddd!" he said, imitating one of the more endearing lines in the movie. I couldn't hold in my reaction anymore and laughed so hard, tears poured down my cheeks. He held me tighter and wiped the tears off my face.

"You're right, Dustin, that was the worst movie I've ever seen," I said.

"I will never look at popcorn the same way again," Joseph said. "Or corn on the cob, for that matter."

"How did that even get made?" Amy asked, her arms flying out.

"Direct to VHS, baby," Dustin said. "It don't get much better than that."

"Yes. Yes, it does." Amy softened and started laughing, too, as she reunited with Dustin in the bean bag. They shifted to face us. "Don't worry, Kincaid. You and I will pick the movie next time."

"It's really fine," I told her. "Now, pretty much every movie I see for the rest of my life will be an improvement over that one."

"Hey, I warned you all it was *that* bad," Dustin said. He kissed Amy on the nose.

"True," Joseph said, taking my hand as footsteps descended on us.

"You kids need anything?" Amy's mom asked from the bottom stair.

"No, Mom, we're good. The movie just ended." Her mom nodded and went back upstairs. "You guys want to hang out here for a little while longer?" Amy asked.

Joseph looked at me and then down at his watch. "Kincaid has to be home by ten." I peeked at his watch. It wasn't even eight o'clock yet. "I guess we can stay for another hour or so."

"I'll go upstairs and find us a game," Amy said, standing up. "Come on, Kincaid. Girl talk." I shrugged my shoulders at the boys and followed her upstairs to her room.

Amy's room looked like a unicorn had exploded in it. There were pink glittery accents everywhere down to the canopy bed and curtain rods. She caught the awe in my eyes. "I know," she said with a giggle. "My mom went a little overboard with the décor, but I didn't want to hurt her feelings." She handed me a stack of board games from the top of her closet and grabbed a second stack for herself, instructing me to put them on the bed. "See anything you want to play?"

"I haven't played a lot of games like this."

"That's too bad," she said. "The boys can get really competitive. It's cute sometimes, and annoying other times." She looked at the games one at a time, placing two off to the side and the others back in her closet. She sat down on the bed and grinned.

"What?" I thought she might start laughing like a hyena.

"You and Joe! Y'all seemed all cozy on the couch."

I tried to hide my smile with my hand, but it was already too late.

"Aww!" she said. "I think it's great! It's too bad you don't live closer."

"Yeah," I said. "But you never know. There's a chance I may have to move here."

"Oh?" She picked up the musical note pendant from her neck and began twirling it between her fingers. "I bet you'd miss your friends at your current school, though. I've been at the same school my whole life."

"Yeah, me too." I looked at her welcoming face and knew I could trust her. "I may not have a choice. My parents...um, well, they might split up."

"I'm sorry," she said, her voice wavering a bit. "I'll pray for them. And you. If you do move here, you can hang out with Heather and me. You'll have friends here. My best friend moved away during elementary. We write letters, but I still miss her. I'm sure your friends would write to you."

"Thanks." I sighed as I looked at the games she'd selected, Connect Four and Battleship. "So, you've known Joseph since kindergarten?"

"Yep. Ever since he, Dustin, and Kevin ran around crying out battle cries of the *Teenage Mutant Ninja Turtles* on the playground."

"They must have been cute doing that as little kids."

"Who said anything about little kids? I'm pretty sure they only stopped last year."

I giggled. "How long have you and Dustin been a couple?"

"Forever," she said dreamily. "And not that long, either. Since the winter formal dance in January. But we've been friends forever. I just never saw him as a brother like I do with Kevin and Joe."

"I can't imagine going out with any of my guy friends back home."

"Of course not, silly. You've only got eyes for Joe now." She stood up and grabbed the games. "Come on. We can't leave them unsupervised for too long, or they'll start talking about us."

Amy paused at the basement door and placed her index finger over her mouth to warn me to be quiet. We tiptoed down the stairs until we could hear the guys talking.

"I don't know what it is," Joseph said. "Not yet."

"Well, you're treating her like she's your girlfriend," Dustin said. "Holding her on the sofa. I could almost hear Amy's girly heart thumping at the sight of it."

"I already told you I like her," Joseph said. "We're dating and getting to know each other."

"Are you dating anyone else?" Dustin paused, and I assumed Joseph was shaking his head. "Do you want to see anyone else?"

"No, I don't."

"Does she?"

Of course not, Joseph! My head was screaming.

"I don't think so, or at least I hope not," Joseph said.

"Dude," Dustin said. "Then she's basically your girlfriend, whether or not you have the balls to ask her to make it official. You kiss her yet?"

I looked at Amy, who grabbed my shoulder with her free hand and bounced up and down on the stairs. "Hey, guys," she said, announcing our presence. "Are you ready to have your butts kicked by a couple of girls?"

"Oh, you know it," Dustin said, taking the games from Amy. "Let's play Battleship. Couples against each other."

Joseph looked up and awkwardly smiled at me as I sat beside him on the couch. Amy moved the bean bag closer to the coffee table while Dustin set up the game. Joseph and I worked together to set up our battleships. After a heated game that lasted nearly an hour, Joseph and I were victorious in sinking Amy and Dustin's ships. By that point, we had to call it a night.

As I rode in Joseph's truck, I knew he had to take me back to the motel, but I wasn't ready for the evening to end. There was a new energy hanging out in the air between us, and I think we both felt it. I'd never felt anything else like it before. I looked out the window at the stars and wondered if they all shared energy like people who were falling in love. If it was love.

"What are you thinking about?" Joseph asked. "You're not usually so quiet."

"The stars."

"There's a lookout point coming up. Do you want to stop for a while?"

My heart jumped into my throat. Those were places teenagers went to make out. We were teenagers. What was he really asking me? I didn't know how to answer. I wanted to see the lookout point, but I was afraid.

He pulled off the road to a darkened spot overlooking the lake. It was as close to the motel as possible without being on my grandparents' property. "You were off in your own world, so I thought I'd stop and show you this place." He rolled down both windows and turned off the engine.

"I'm sorry. I was just…"

"Scared?" Joseph slid next to me. "It's all right." He put his arm around me and pulled me closer. All the hairs on my arms stood up, which made me shiver, even though it was still hot and humid outside.

I leaned my head against his shoulder and closed my eyes. I wasn't really afraid of him. The whole situation scared me. I'd never been in love before, but I was certain it was happening to me. People always described it as butterflies in their stomachs, tingling sensations down to their toes, exhilaration, and longing to be with the person—not overwhelming confusion and fear of the unknown mixed with nausea.

"I don't bite, you know," Joseph said. "I just want to show you the stars."

"I love stars," I said. "They're beautiful."

He laughed and caressed my cheek. "They're a lot prettier if you actually look at them."

I opened my eyes and found myself staring into his. Like magnets drawn together, our lips connected for the kiss I'd craved all evening. Everything was perfect—the warm breeze, the scent of the lake water, and Joseph's gentle hands, one on my cheek and the other on the small of my back—until a sports car pulled up beside my window, rattling with obnoxious music blaring from inside it. Joseph stopped kissing me and glared at the guy in the car who was rolling down his window. I recognized him from the pizza place.

"Oooh!" the guy called, continuing to whoop and holler. "Little Joey virgin has himself a girlfriend! Ain't nobody getting lucky here tonight, sweetheart! You should come over here with me." I turned to Joseph, shocked by the guy's forwardness.

Joseph mouthed to me, "I'm so sorry," and then he leaned over me to reach the window. "Why don't you get out of here, James, and leave us alone? We're not bothering you or anyone else."

"This place is only for people who get action!" James responded.

Joseph smiled at him. "James, I know you're still having a hard time since your girlfriend dumped you in front of the whole school, but you can't take it out on everyone else. *My* girlfriend and I will give you privacy to take care of that *action* on your own. Have a good evening." I couldn't believe the quickness with which the insult rolled off Joseph's tongue, which only seconds ago had briefly touched my own.

James stuttered a bit, trying to think of a comeback as Joseph rolled up our windows but said nothing and finally stuck his middle finger out the window at Joseph. Joseph just waved and smiled at him as he started his truck.

"Old friend of yours?" I asked as Joseph slowly backed out of the gravel lot.

"If by 'friend' you mean the biggest prick in the whole school, then, yeah; Jamie-boy and I go way back. We were friends in elementary." As Joseph backed out, his truck's headlights illuminated the hateful stickers that adorned the car's back bumper. Then, Joseph spoke my lesson for the day.

Lesson 26: Some assholes leave it a mystery until you talk to them. Others make it abundantly clear by putting a "No Fat Chicks" sticker on their cars.

We stayed silent for the next few minutes as Joseph drove me back to the motel. I wondered what he was thinking and if James had upset him. All I could think about was the fact that he'd referred to me as his girlfriend. Wasn't it too soon? Maybe, but it was probably too soon for me to think I was falling in love with him.

Joseph stopped the truck near my room and turned off the engine. My grandparents were watching us from their doorway. They waved at us as Joseph and I got out of the truck, and then they went inside, turning off their light.

"I'm sorry about James being a dick like that and even sorrier you had to see me be a dick back to him," Joseph said as we reached my door. "That's not usually how I am, I promise."

"It's okay," I said, taking his hand. "I don't think he understands anything but dick-talk, and he started it."

Joseph laughed and hugged me, breathing in as if he were trying to inhale my hair. "Oh, Kincaid, I love…" he pulled away as I gasped. He looked terrified. "I love spending time with you. You're fun to be around, and I like you so much."

"I like you too," I said softly, meeting his approaching lips halfway. He lifted me a few inches off the ground and made my head swim in the process. I left my arms around his neck as he put me down. "Did you mean what you said to James?"

"Which part?" He smirked at me.

"When you said I was your…" I couldn't even get the word out; I felt too silly and self-conscious. I buried my face in his chest and felt his arms tighten around me, the only sensation grounding me and saving me from utter humiliation.

Joseph took my head and kissed me. "Yes," he said. "I want you to be my girlfriend officially. Will you? And you won't hurt my feelings if you think it's too soon. I don't want to pressure you to—"

I cut him off with another kiss as he started to ramble, hoping he'd stop talking long enough to kiss me back, which he did. After I pulled away, I just stared at him, his eyes sparkling in the light above us. "Yes, boyfriend," I said. "Goodnight."

He embraced me for one last hug before he went back to his truck, stumbling on a rock as he walked away. I stepped backward into my room and locked the door, leaning against it for a moment to catch my breath. As I threw myself on the bed, I grabbed a pillow and screamed into it while kicking my feet in the air. The rest of the summer would be the best one of my whole life. I could just feel something even more amazing happening soon.

Chapter 23

I dragged myself off the bed and paced in my room. At exactly ten-thirty, the phone rang, and I dove across the bed to answer it before the ringing could disturb the guest next door.

"Courtney, oh, my God, I have so much to tell you!" I answered. "But you first, what's up with you?"

"Are you freakin' kidding me? I've been babysitting. End of story. Tell me how things are going with Joseph!"

"We totally had the boyfriend-girlfriend conversation tonight after our date, and then he kissed me like I want to be kissed every time for the rest of my life!"

Courtney squealed so loudly I had to hold the phone away from my ear until she quieted down. "This is so big! You have an actual boyfriend after meeting the guy a few weeks ago! I love you, but I hate you too!"

"It'll happen for you too, Court."

"Just not with any of the boys at our school."

"I know. Gross. All the nice boys feel like our brothers anyway. There's more…"

"More what?"

"I think I'm falling in love with him." Silence followed, which reminded me of those phone company commercials that boasted calls so clear you could hear a pin drop. I sat up to make sure the call button was still lit up on the phone. "Courtney? Are you still there?"

"Yes. Just give me a minute to process. That's a really big deal, Kincaid. Shit! Love, already? Are you sure?"

She was right; I was probably crazy. I rehashed everything that had happened between Joseph and me, not breaking his confidence about his secret. I waited in agony for Courtney's expert analysis. I'm not sure why I thought she'd know more about love than me when I was the one feeling it.

"I think you're definitely infatuated, girl," she concluded. "Just don't jump in too fast. I don't want you to get your heart broken again, like with Derek."

"Derek who?" I retorted.

Courtney chuckled. The rest of our call wasn't so lighthearted since I told her about Ed's death. She was sympathetic, but I knew Ed's death wouldn't affect Courtney as much as it had affected me.

After flipping through all the channels and finding nothing, I got up and ran a bubble bath. Something about a bubble bath always made me feel better no matter what was bothering me. I remembered something Ed had told me about writers needing solitude and time to soak in their thoughts as much as they needed companionship. I figured soaking in my thoughts could happen more easily if I was also soaking in the tub.

I felt like Ed had gifted me with a lifetime of writing passion during our hours of conversation. I missed our talks by the lake. My grandparents were around the same age as Ed. I wondered how much longer they'd live. My other grandparents had died during the same year when I was six or maybe seven. They couldn't live without each other. Just like Ed couldn't live without Rosa. Nothing like my parents.

Did love like that even exist anymore? Maybe Courtney was right. I didn't know anything about love, but Ed had known.

Dragging myself out of the now lukewarm water, I dried off and slipped into an oversized nightshirt. I combed my hair and grabbed my glasses off the vanity as I went back to my bed. Inside the nightstand drawer lay Ed's notebook. I had been too sad to open it before.

With my face several inches above the book, I inhaled the scent of the old leather and worn, yellowed pages. I reread Ed's poem for Rosa in the front and wiped tears from my eyes with my shirt to protect the delicate pages. There was a navy-blue ribbon marking a spot in the book that I turned to next.

Dear daughter,
I hear your voice in the wind on this lonely prairie
Telling me to stop calling.
Your mother prays for you here—
A pink desert rose clashing with the burnt-orange dunes.
As we walk hand in hand, seeking you,
You run farther out of our grasps—
A landlocked pearl, too delicate for our grit,
Thrown back into the ocean.

Having read all of Ed's published work, it was nothing I'd seen before. The imagery intrigued me as I imagined the feel of the wind against my face and the gritty prairie dust pelting my skin. A daughter? Ed and Rosa had no children. Was it a metaphorical daughter? The pink desert rose had to symbolize Rosa, but the landlocked pearl thrown back into the ocean? What did it all mean?

Realizing it was past midnight, I encased Ed's notebook in a hand towel, treating it as though it might explode if I jostled it too much as I hid it back in the nightstand drawer.

"Ed," I said toward the window. "What were you trying to tell me?"

My dreams were plagued with images of a younger Ed (like the photos in his book jackets) with a beautiful dark-haired woman with curly hair flowing down her back. On a ship, they dropped something that resembled an oyster shell over the railings as they watched the sunset.

I was jolted awake by thunder rattling the windows, and then lightning lit up the room. I shivered and pulled the quilt up to my chin like I used to when I was a little girl. As thunder roared again, I sat up in bed. Ed and Rosa had lost a child, their daughter. They were more like my parents than I'd realized.

"Oh, Ed," I whispered. "I'm so sorry." More lightning shot across the sky, the zagged streaks visible through my thick drapes. I jumped up and opened the connecting door to my grandparents' apartment and climbed back into bed under the safety of my quilt. "Patrick, I miss you, and I know Mom and Dad do too. God, please help them love each other again just like Ed and Rosa did."

Lesson 27: *People are capable of hiding more pain than we realize.*

Chapter 24

When I woke up the next morning, the adjoining door to my room was closed, but I could smell bacon cooking from Grandma's kitchen. Not bothering to change out of my pajamas, I slipped on a bra and combed through my messy hair at the bathroom vanity. I grabbed my glasses and headed to their apartment.

I froze in my tracks when I found Joseph sitting at the table with my grandparents. "Hi," I said to him, trying not to blush too much. "Good morning, Grandma and Grandpa."

"Hey there, sweetie," Grandma said, placing a plate in front of the empty chair beside Joseph. "Quite the storm we had last night, huh?"

"It was. My windows rattled every time it thundered." I sat down beside Joseph, and he smiled at me.

"I closed your door this morning so we wouldn't disturb you," Grandpa said. "I guess you've outgrown crawling into bed between us during thunderstorms, huh?"

Joseph chuckled.

Geez, did Grandpa have to say such embarrassing things in front of my boyfriend? Had Joseph told them?

"We lost a tree last night," Joseph said. "It took out a small part of the fence, but at least it missed the roof."

I turned to him. "That must have been scary. I'm glad you didn't get hurt."

"I'm tougher than that," he said with a grin. "I didn't even hear it fall over all the thunder."

"I didn't even know it was supposed to storm last night."

"Heat storm," Grandpa interjected. "Damn things pop up sometimes during hot summer nights and scare the piss out of you."

"Do you think you could come help me with my fence today, Kincaid?" Joseph asked. "If it's okay with Mr. and Mrs. Kincaid."

"I don't know," Grandpa said to Grandma with a wink. "Can we trust these two to stop playing kissy face long enough to accomplish the work?"

This is how my life will end, I thought. *I will literally drop dead from embarrassment with a piece of bacon still clutched between my teeth.*

"Chester!" Grandma scolded. "You're making the poor kids blush. It's fine for you to go with Joseph, Kincaid. Your grandpa and I have to talk to Ed's attorney on the phone later this morning."

Joseph waited in my grandparents' apartment while I managed to shower and dress within ten minutes. I was anxious to see where this boy—my boyfriend—lived. The fact that we'd be there alone was an added bonus. I hoped there'd be time for more kissing after the fence work was done.

After driving for what felt like forever, Joseph turned off the main highway onto a long dirt road that seemed deserted. There were no houses in sight, only overgrown fields with rusted barbed-wire fences lining their front borders and thick trees along the back. In the distance, smoke billowed from behind the tree line.

"Joseph…"

He glanced over and grinned. "Don't worry. It's just my neighbors clearing some brush. They're planning to build a house and tear down the two older houses on their property. Dane's dad used to rent a house out here."

"So that's where it was. Sylvia told me about Dane's dad the day she dyed Veronica's hair. It was a pretty sad story, the way he ran off like that."

"I don't really know either side of it, but neither of us knows what happened with Dane's dad. Sylvia never had the chance to tell him about Dane, so the guy doesn't even know he has a son. It's sad for him too."

"But he chose to leave her. He shouldn't have acted like he loved her if he didn't. There's no sense in that. It's no wonder everyone thinks love is stupid." I crossed my arms and looked out the window as Joseph pulled up beside a grey mailbox on a metal pole. He pulled out the mail and tossed it in the seat between as we continued down the bumpy driveway.

His house was a brick ranch-style home with a double carport and a front porch the length of the house. He pulled into the carport and got out, practically running around the front of the truck to get to my door before I could open it. He reached across my lap to unbuckle my seatbelt and retrieve the envelopes and catalogs from the seat. After he had tossed the mail onto the porch, he wrapped his arms around my waist and dragged me out of the truck, lifting me onto the porch.

"What are you doing?" I asked, crossing my arms again. "You're going to hurt your back!"

He stepped up beside me. "You're not heavy." He pulled me into a hug, leaving my arms between us, and kissed my forehead. "And love isn't stupid. I get what you're saying about feeling bad for Sylvia, but I can't just condemn a guy I've never met when I don't know the whole story."

Joseph was too compassionate, and I was still a jerk. Maybe I hadn't learned anything at all so far. I freed my arms and hugged him back, resting my head against his chest. "I'm sorry," I said. "You're right."

"Come on," he said. "I'll show you the house first so we can get some water before we get started on the fence. It shouldn't take too long. I just have to reset a couple of posts in concrete and patch the broken parts of the chain-link."

"Does this mean I get to see your room?"

"Only if you promise not to laugh at me for being such a dork. I still have a lot of toys on display from when I was a kid."

"Aren't we still kids?" I poked him in the stomach with my index finger, tickling him slightly. "Sort of..."

He seized my hand to stop the tickling. "Stop it!" he said, running away from me toward the front door. "I'm extremely ticklish!"

I chased after him. "I could use this new-found knowledge for evil!" He managed to hold me back, and we laughed while he unlocked his house. As he kicked the door closed behind us, I went in for one last tickle-attack on his stomach, sending us both tumbling onto the floor after tripping over a padded ottoman. We both burst into laughter again before he dragged himself onto the couch. He helped me up, too, and we lay there, exhausted from our fit of laughter.

"Truce?" he said, trying his best to give me a sad puppy-dog face.

I laughed. "Of course," I said, looking up at him and not realizing until that moment half of my body was trapped under his. I was nervous, not because I was afraid of him or anything, but because I wasn't at all afraid of the situation in which we'd found ourselves.

"We should probably get that water now."

"Probably."

"You're not trying to get up."

"Neither are you," I said. "You've kind of got me trapped here."

"Oh, God!" he said. "I've got to be hurting you!"

"You're not. I'm fine." I leaned up to kiss him, wrapping my arms around his neck to pull him closer. He kissed me back immediately, sending waves of electricity shooting through my body. *What am I doing!* My conscience screamed at me to stop before things went too far, but it also reminded me of Joseph's purity pledge. I became hypersensitive to where his hands were—one stretched out above our heads and the other holding my head, his thumb tickling my cheek. He moved one hand to my waist, keeping it on top of my shirt and never attempted to move it higher or lower.

I suddenly understood what all those older girls at my school whispered about in the bathrooms. One thing leading to another and another. I was just about to pull away when Joseph stopped kissing me and sat up, moving to the other end of the couch as fast as he could manage. He hugged a throw pillow, cramming it into his lap, and rested his face in his hands. I knew all the reasons we needed to stop, but I still felt terrible and rejected at the same time. Willing my body to take up as little space as possible on the other end of the couch, I sat up, too, as tears welled up in my eyes.

Joseph exhaled and looked at me. "Kincaid..." He moved closer, reaching for me as I backed away.

"Did I do something wrong?" Tears spilled down my cheeks.

"No...please, don't cry." He brought the pillow with him as he moved closer. He took my hand and kissed it like a gentleman from one of those Jane Austin novel-based movies Courtney liked to watch. "Come here," he said, offering to hold me against his shoulder. I inched closer and tucked myself under his arm, my knees still pressed against my chest. "Nothing's wrong. We just both needed to calm down a bit, don't you think?" He kissed the top of my head and sighed, still short of breath from our make-out session.

"No, I did something wrong when we were making out, and you have to tell me what it was so I don't do it again. If you even want to do that again...with me, I mean. Oh, God." My cheeks burned over my throbbing jaws as I fought back tears of humiliation.

"*You* did nothing wrong, Kincaid. *We* did nothing wrong. It's just...well...just because my heart and my brain tell me to wait...my body didn't get the message at that moment. I had to stop before we kept going and went too far if you get what I mean..."

OH. MY. GOD. He stopped because I, awkward and mouthy Kincaid Walsh, had turned him on. It should have been blatantly obvious to me when he'd shoved the pillow in his lap. I might have been a virgin, but it didn't mean I knew nothing at all about sex and how the parts worked. I buried my head in his chest to hide my face.

"I'm all sweaty," Joseph whispered, patting me on the back.

"I don't care," I mumbled. "I'm so embarrassed; I should have figured it out without having to ask. I'm so naïve. Feel free to dump me now."

He kissed the top of my head and held me. "I don't want to dump you. I want to keep getting embarrassed with you." I forced myself to face him. "I really, really, like you, Kincaid." He brushed my hair behind my ears and kissed me so softly, it felt like a butterfly dancing on my lips.

"I really, really like you too." I closed my eyes and sat in silence with Joseph. We held hands and waited until both our heart rates had returned to normal twenty minutes later.

Lesson 28: Not all boys have only one thing on their minds.

Chapter 25

J oseph's room was everything I'd imagined, now that I felt like he was letting me know the real him. Everything was in a masculine color scheme of navy, tan, and red, down to the plaid wallpaper above the paneling on the lower half of the walls. An unmade full-sized bed sat against one wall near a simple chest with a couple of framed photos on top. Posters of rock bands featured in my own bedroom back home decorated his double closet doors. Art supplies lay scattered on a drawing table in the corner of the room near a large window overlooking the backyard.

I walked to the chest to study the photos. A family camping trip with his parents that looked to be a couple of years old and a studio portrait of the family when Joseph must have been five or six. "These are really great photos."

Joseph leaned against the doorframe. "Yeah, I like to keep them close. Now that I think about it, their wedding photo is still in the entryway. Veronica thinks I look like our dad, but I don't see it."

"I do." I held the frame as if it were the most fragile thing in the world. "Right here." I pointed to his father's cheek. "When you smile—like really smile—you have the same cute little dimple." He blushed and shook his head as I put down the photo.

"I guess we should get to work, huh?"

I sighed. "If we have to."

It was terribly hot outside, but luckily, the broken fence area was still under some shade trees. I helped clear the debris and smaller twigs from the fallen tree. It wasn't a large tree, but it still did quite a bit of damage when it crashed into the backyard. Joseph impressed me with his ease and precision of operating the gas-powered chainsaw he pulled from his shed. Once the tree was cut into firewood, we surveyed the damage on the fence.

One section was completely flattened to the ground with two supporting posts bent almost in half. The rest of the fence seemed fine, unaffected by the storm. Joseph cut the wires still holding the pieces together and tried to wiggle the bent posts. I stepped in to help and exhausted myself pulling on the posts.

"Hold up," Joseph said. He ran over to the large gate near the house and swung open the sides. "I'll use my truck to pull out the posts. I'll need it to pull out the tree stump anyway."

As I waited, I looked around the yard. An abandoned metal swing set sat at the back corner across from what appeared to be a dilapidated fort near some pine trees. Under the back patio sat a medium-sized dog house. A couple of tennis balls rested outside the dog's space inside an empty bowl, but there was no sign of a dog except for the still-full water dish.

Joseph's truck came roaring through the gates. I stepped aside and stayed out of his way as he backed up near the posts. He pulled some chains from a small storage closet at the back of his house. I loved the way his arms flexed as he wrapped the chains tight around the poles and attached the ends to his trailer hitch. He caught me watching him and grinned as he lifted his hat and wiped the sweat off his forehead. I still had no clue what to do with a boyfriend, but Joseph didn't seem to mind when I met him with a kiss as he stood up. Part of me was worried he'd push me away.

"What was that for?" he asked, turning his hat around backward. I'd always had a thing for boys in hats. His dimples distracted me, and my knees went weak. I tripped and fell against him. "Whoa, there, clumsy girlfriend."

I just laughed. "I don't know how the hell to be a girlfriend, Joseph. All I do is embarrass myself." And even though every mistake I made around him was excruciating, he seemed unbothered by my awkwardness.

"I don't know how to be a boyfriend either, but I think we'll figure it out."

"How will we figure it out if I don't end up moving here?"

"The same way we'll figure it out if you do, just with more distance between us. And you don't have the monopoly on being embarrassed. I'm the one who got a hard-on when we made out for the first time."

I blushed. "Yeah, I guess that was pretty embarrassing…"

"At least we can be embarrassed and awkward together."

Working together, we installed new posts and patched the broken links in the fence with flexible metal pieces that Joseph expertly bent and twisted into the right shape. He said he'd attach the sections of fencing to the posts after the concrete had set later that evening. We sat on the tailgate of his truck and admired our handiwork. I had to admit, it felt good working with my hands.

"Hey, Joseph, where's your dog?" I asked, pointing to the dog house. "And what kind is it?"

"She's staying with Todd at his parents' house until the fence is fixed. Good thing I let her sleep inside in my room last night because of the storm. Her name's Taffy. She's a blond mixed breed we adopted almost six years ago when I'd finally convinced my dad that, at ten years old, I was responsible enough to take care of one. She's small like a beagle, but even the vet can't determine exactly what kind of dog she is. Says her parents were probably mutts too."

"Aww, I want to meet her. I love dogs, but Mom and Dad never would let me have one."

"It seems weird being out here without throwing a tennis ball for her."

"I bet you do miss her."

"Oh, she's getting plenty of loving today," he said with a chuckle. "Todd's little sister's keeping her entertained. She's trying to get her parents on board with getting a dog, so this is her day of practice. She's a lot younger than Todd. I think she just turned nine or maybe ten."

When I turned to Joseph, he was grinning at me. "What?" I checked to see if I had a bug on me or something.

"Nothing. You're just so cute with a hat and your hair all messy sticking out the back of it."

"So, you prefer this to the way I dress for church?"

"Honestly, yeah. This is you to me. Casual, with no makeup on and your glasses. Here…" He caressed my cheek. "And inside too."

Obviously, the best response I had after that was a kiss. It was also the moment I realized we were no longer alone.

"Hey, Joe," a gruff male voice called. "Thought you might need help with the fence, but I see you're busy." The gruffness resolved into a lighthearted chuckle.

I jumped back and turned toward the voice. A short, older guy in his forties stood at the fence gate. He wore torn jeans and an old flannel shirt with the sleeves cut off. I couldn't tell if his frizzy hair was natural or he'd styled it that way because it stood at least three inches off the top of his head.

"I could use help dragging the stump the rest of the way out of the ground, Mr. Henderson," Joseph called back. He turned back to me. "That's my neighbor; he's a game warden. He's the one burning all the brush across the field."

Mr. Henderson walked around the fence's perimeter and stopped near the stump that had been slightly ripped from the ground. "Best thing we can do is pull it out with your truck. You're right that it's too close to your fence to burn it out."

Joseph agreed and drove his truck around to meet his neighbor. He introduced me to Mr. Henderson, and then both guys stood together, silently staring at the stump to decide the best angle of approach. No matter what they did, there'd be a hole to fill according to their discussion. Somehow, they got the bright idea that I should drive the truck so they could watch the stump being pulled from the ground. What fascinated them about it, I had no idea, but I agreed since Joseph's truck was an automatic. Had it been a manual, I couldn't have helped. Manual vehicles freaked me out.

As soon as I got the go-ahead from Mr. Henderson, I put the truck into drive and drove into the field until I felt the slack in the chain snap. The tires spun a bit, but I kept going at Joseph's urging and felt the slack return to the chain as the roots gave way and ripped the stump from the ground. I drove the truck a bit farther before I put it in park and turned off the engine. When I got out of the truck, Joseph and Mr. Henderson were staring into the hole that remained. Joseph was paler than I'd ever seen him as he held his cap in his hands. Neither of them spoke as I approached, wiping sweat from my brow.

"What's going on?" I asked, my voice penetrating Joseph's daze only after I'd repeated my question.

His eyes met mine, and he said flatly, "Holy shit, Kincaid, there's a dead body buried in my backyard."

Chapter 26

I peered into the hole as slowly as possible to see what Joseph and Mr. Henderson were gaping at, not sure I wanted to. *A dead body? What the hell was I thinking by looking into the hole?* I let out a gasp as I looked down. Even without my brief fascination with mummies and all things Egyptian when I was in fifth grade, I couldn't have mistaken the bones for an animal. A human skull and torso lay twisted in the ground, still partially covered by dirt.

Finally, the adult in our group took charge and pulled a radio off the side of his belt. He asked the person on the other end to send the police to Joseph's house and waited with us. "Don't touch anything," he advised. "Just go sit."

We opened Joseph's tailgate and sat, staring at the hole in the yard. Joseph bowed his head and mouthed some words as I leaned against his shoulder. He raised up and put his arm around my shoulders when he'd finished. Noticing my puzzled expression, he explained himself. "I was saying a prayer for the family of whoever it is. It doesn't look like a natural burial."

"What are you saying?" I asked. "Murder?"

Joseph nodded.

Mr. Henderson knelt beside the hole and whistled before he spoke. "Sweetheart, your boy's onto something. This skull's been crushed by a blunt object. I've seen the same type of injuries on the skulls of animals who've been killed by clubs or baseball bats by people defending themselves with what's available during attacks. This was no natural death, and I'd be willing to bet this body's been here no longer than twenty years or so."

I stood up to join him and listened as he pointed out the scraps of leather from the belt the victim had been wearing. The skull was clearly dented on one side, and the mouth was open in a way that suggested a scream. I got chills just looking at it. Then I saw it—the thing that turned my chills into a cold sweat and lightheadedness. As I scanned the rest of the dirt and gravel near the victim's head, I saw the shark tooth necklace exactly as it had appeared in Sylvia's photograph of Mitch. I covered my mouth and backed away, fighting the urge to be sick.

Joseph jumped up and grabbed my arms to steady me as I stumbled. "Kincaid, are you okay?"

I couldn't speak at first; all I could do was cry. Joseph hugged me tightly until we heard vehicles pulling into the driveway. Mr. Henderson walked around the front of the house to lead the officers our way, and I managed to untie my tongue for a moment. "Sylvia," I said. "Aunt Sylvia's Mitch."

"Oh, God," Joseph said.

"What?" Mr. Henderson asked from behind me. "What are you talking about? Who's Mitch?" Two police officers stood behind him.

I dried my face. "Mitch. My cousin's father who left before he was born. The necklace buried in there is just like the one he wore in the only photo of him my Aunt Sylvia has. He didn't leave them; he was murdered."

And with that, Joseph was pale again. He put me back on the tailgate of his truck as other officials descended on the area.

Lesson 29: Things are not always as they seem.

My grandparents arrived soon after the police. Word must have traveled fast because, in the haze of all the things going on around me, a line of yellow tape had been placed around the area to keep out the steady stream of onlookers.

"Police scanner," Joseph said, pulling me away from my thoughts. "That's all some people do around here is listen to the police scanner to hear some gossip on who's getting in trouble. Usually, it's drunk and disorderly stuff."

"I guess a murder victim is more sensational for them." My words came out angrier than I'd expected. I was still reeling from the statement I'd given the old police officer who had arrived first. He'd looked at me like I was crazy when I told him I had an idea of who the victim was. The officer had wondered aloud as he scratched his large gut how many of those fake shark-tooth necklaces were around after *Jaws* came out. He didn't have to make me feel like an idiot. "I just know it's Mitch."

Joseph pulled me into a hug. "Hey, it's going to be okay."

After I'd given my statement to yet another officer, I was allowed to step outside of the barrier into the comfort of my grandmother's outstretched arms. "Oh, sweetheart," she said. "Seeing something like that must have terrified you."

"Seeing a human skeleton changes a person," Grandpa said, more to the onlookers than to me. "You folks should go on home." He ushered me to his car as Todd and Veronica arrived.

Todd waited outside the police tape while Veronica motioned for Joseph to come closer. She hugged him over the barrier, and he began recounting the story to her as my grandfather helped my grandmother into the car. Joseph waved at me slightly as we pulled out. It wasn't how I'd expected my day with him to end.

I had to retell the story to my grandparents during our drive back to the motel. At least they didn't dismiss my concerns about whose skeleton was buried in Joseph's yard.

"A bunch of shady rent houses used to occupy the area across from the Bennett property," Grandpa said. "Shrooms and other drugs sold and bartered according to some men I shoot the shit with down at the ol' barbershop. I guess Sylvia got herself in with some heathens back in the day if that body's Dane's father."

"Now, Ches, we have no idea that our girl did anything more than fall in love with the wrong boy back then," Grandma scolded. "What does that teach Kincaid about not judging others till she's walked in their shoes?"

"I'm sorry, but shroomers and potheads don't need breaks from judging," he said. "The Good Lord'll take care of 'em someday if they've not all OD'd and faced Him already."

"Exactly!" Grandma exclaimed. "Leave the judging to the Good Lord."

Grandpa scoffed and turned up the radio to hear Johnny Cash singing "Ring of Fire." At least I could prepare myself for facing Sylvia. Someone needed to tell her, and somehow, I knew it would be me.

Sylvia walked out of the main office when we got back. She stood with her hand on her hip watching us as we piled out of the car. "You just can't catch a break, kiddo," she said to me. I shrugged, giving myself a few more seconds to think of what to say. Until I said something, she still thought Mitch was alive and well. She thought he'd left her and Dane—not that Mitch had known about his son at the time. Would knowing he was dead help her or make it worse?

"Hon, will you please come into the apartment with us for a bit?" Grandma asked. "Kincaid and I have something to tell you."

Instantly, Sylvia's sympathetic smile turned to concern as she followed her parents. I brought up the rear, closing the door behind me as I noticed a police car crawling slowly into the parking lot near the walking trails.

"What's wrong, Kincaid?" Grandpa asked. Apparently, my poker-face needed work.

"Police." My voice came out cracked and quieter than I'd expected.

Grandpa stood up as Sylvia asked, "What's going on, and why do I get the feeling this involves me?"

"I'll go talk to the officers and let you girls talk real quick," Grandpa said, leaving the apartment.

"Mom? Kincaid?"

I looked at Grandma, who squeezed my knee and urged me to speak. I wasn't sure I could, but I pulled every ounce of strength I had to open my mouth and tell her what I'd seen at Joseph's house. Sylvia's eyes became glassy as I told her about the shark necklace and why I thought the body might have been Mitch.

She covered her nose and mouth with her hands, leaning against them in a prayer-stance. "Oh, my God!" she cried. "This can't be happening. I need time to think about all this." She took a deep, shaky breath as her face drained of all color.

The door opened, startling all of us. Grandpa walked in with two officers following him, a man who looked to be my dad's age and a woman who looked barely older than me.

"Sylvia," the male officer said.

"Martin," Sylvia said. *They knew each other. What did that mean? Would he go easy on her, play the good cop? Was he a good cop?*

Officer Martin looked at me and then back at Sylvia, who was on the verge of falling apart—I could just tell. I recognized Martin from Joseph's house. "We need to speak to you. Would you like to talk here or down at the station?"

"Here's fine," Sylvia said.

"May we speak in private?" the female officer interjected. She sounded like a perky babysitter trying her best to act solemn in a school play.

The loudest and most excruciating silence I'd ever known filled the air. I could almost feel the weight of it crushing me as I backed out of the room, closing the front door behind me. A moment later, Grandma and Grandpa came outside too. The three of us silently shuffled toward the walking trail.

A million thoughts came to mind. Would Sylvia be okay if it was Mitch's skeleton Joseph and I had found? How would Dane react? Was it an accident or was it murder? If he was murdered, who killed him? Holy shit. In movies, the first suspect was always the jilted lover. Would Sylvia be accused of murder? Surely, the police would know she wasn't capable of such a thing. Wouldn't they?

I kept my slow pace behind Grandma and Grandpa, watching them hold hands as they walked. When they stopped at a bench in the shade, I stood near them under a tree. It was the hottest part of the day, and I would have much rather been inside, or swimming in the lake, or kissing Joseph. How could I even be thinking of kissing Joseph after how the day had progressed, but who was I kidding? I always wanted to kiss him.

"I'm sure everything will be fine, Kincaid," Grandma said, looking up at me, halting my thoughts of Joseph for a moment. "Sylvia's a tough woman. I don't think she did anything wrong."

"I know."

"They're probably only talking to her because of Kincaid's insistence that the body's that old boyfriend of hers," Grandpa said.

"Grandpa, the shark tooth necklace was what made me think that. How was I supposed to know there were a ton of those made after that stupid movie?"

"I ain't saying you're wrong, darlin' child," he said. "Just offering up an explanation. The boy was a drifter from what I understand. They need Sylvia to identify any other items that might've been with the remains and to contact the boy's family about burial or cremation arrangements."

"After they confirm it's really him."

"They'll excavate the whole area, check for ID and stuff," Grandma said. "And they'll check dental records to make sure. Then they'll find the killer and have someone like Andy Griffith from that *Matlock* lawyer-program to make sure justice is done."

"Grandma, I think Matlock defends people accused of murder. He's not a prosecutor."

"She don't care as long as the lawyer looks like Griffith." Grandpa looked at Grandma, who was grinning at him. "She thinks I kinda look like him sometimes." They kissed—a big, loud smack on the lips. It was nauseating and sweet simultaneously.

I wanted what they had. Soon, I was thinking about Joseph again. I don't know that I ever thought of anyone actually being attracted to me. Joseph had wanted me earlier on the couch. Really wanted me. I'd wanted him, too, but not yet. It was too soon. Knowing what all had happened with Sylvia and her struggle to raise Dane while in an abusive marriage so she wouldn't be alone confirmed in my mind what Joseph had done with his pledge. I didn't want to disappoint my parents, either. I had my own pledge in my heart to wait. Part of me knew then—I wanted to wait for Joseph.

The police were leaving as we got back from our walk. Sylvia stood on the porch, pale and shaking as she clung to the wooden post. I didn't know what to do, but Grandma took Sylvia's hands in hers and led her back inside. I followed them and watched Sylvia collapse on the couch in tears. Grandma held Sylvia's head in her lap while Grandpa went to the kitchen. I stood awkwardly in the center of the room until Grandma motioned for me to sit down in the chair.

Sylvia cried into Grandma's lap. I felt like I should leave the room, but at the same time, I didn't want to disturb anyone by moving. I'd never seen an adult sob so loudly, wailing like an animal in pain. The whole scene caused a lump in my throat and tears to well up in my eyes. The whistle from the tea kettle seemed to reset the noise level in the house as Sylvia's crying subsided.

"Shh," Grandma whispered. "Just get it all out, baby. Everything's going to be all right. This, too, shall pass."

"I—I thought I'd already gotten over him years ago, but now he's really gone," Sylvia choked. "It feels like he just left me yesterday again."

I had to speak up; my voice caught in my throat. "Aunt Sylvia, we don't know that. I'm probably wrong. I'm always wrong…" I'd never wanted so badly to be wrong in my entire life.

"Not this time, Kaykay," she sobbed. "The police were questioning me about my relationship with Mitch. His wallet was still in his pocket when he was killed. They found it with the ID still preserved inside the leather. It's Mitch. My Mitch who had an engagement ring in his wallet with a tiny note: 'Sylvia, please marry me.'"

She burst into tears again, her face seeming to crumble before us. Grandma took Sylvia back in her arms and rocked her gently back and forth.

"Oh, dear," Grandma said. "Dane's father. The boy you loved."

Sylvia sniffled as she nodded.

Grandpa walked in with a cup of tea that he handed to Sylvia. He patted me on the head and retreated back to the kitchen.

Sylvia dried her face, which seemed pointless to me. As soon as her cheeks were dry, more tears fell to wet them again. "The man, Mom. The man I loved more than I loved myself who I thought hadn't loved me. All these years, and he didn't leave me on purpose. Someone killed him, and we never got to be together. He never got to know his son."

"Now, now, dear," Grandma said, blotting Sylvia's face and grabbing her shoulders hard enough to shake her. "From where Mitch has been sitting all these years, I imagine he knows his son quite well; why that boy's got himself his very own guardian angel. And you did, too, dear. I know how mean that scoundrel husband was from what Dane's told me recently. Mitch watched over you to keep that low-life bastard from hitting you. If me or Dad had known, we'd have run over the bastard ourselves. We can't go questioning the Good Lord's motives no matter how bad we want to sometimes."

"But why…"

"Because He knows why, and it's not for us to know in this life. I had to hold your sister—my dear child—while she mourned the loss of her firstborn, all the while grieving that precious boy myself. Oh, I'll admit I was damn mad at Him that day, but never once did I doubt Patrick was in a better place thanks to our Lord, all cured from that damn awful disease. Maybe the Lord saved Mitch from something much worse in the future. Maybe his pain was gone in an instant, and he passed peacefully."

I gasped, and Sylvia's tears stopped like a switch had been flipped. "I never thought about it like that," she said.

"Now, you do," Grandma said, matter-of-factly. "You mourn tonight, and then tomorrow, you get up and dust yourself off. You tell Dane about his father. All the happy times you had with him and that he loved you. Would have loved you both, you hear?"

Sylvia nodded and hugged Grandma as I backed out of the living room into my room. Never had I heard my grandmother speak that way, so confident and prophetic. Despite her obvious effect on Aunt Sylvia, I felt sick to my stomach.

Once in my room, I went out the front door, letting it slam behind me. I ran all the way to the end of the walking trail and several strides past it, deep into the trees. I didn't know where I was going, but I knew I had to get away. When my side started catching, I stopped near a tree and dropped to the ground on my knees. My eyes stung with tears.

Without warning, a memory flooded my mind.

I see my mother from the side, her body folded on the floor, much like I was now. She sobs and wails. Another figure, larger than her—my dad—hovers over her before collapsing to the floor beside her. He wraps her in his arms. I stand in a doorway, leaning against the frame, not knowing what to do. My favorite stuffed animal, a monkey with long arms, dangles from my hand, its feet dragging on the carpet. I am cold and scared. A man crouches in front

*of me and wipes tears from my face before scooping me up
in his arms. Grandpa. He carries me down the hallway.
Over his shoulder, I see the hospital bed where my brother
sleeps. A lady behind him in a white shirt disconnects a
machine that has a green line running across the center.*

It was the first time I'd remembered the exact day of
my brother's death. All the tears I'd ever suppressed in
my whole life seemed to pour out of me all at once. I
couldn't stop them, even as I gagged and dry-heaved
near the ground.

Minutes, or maybe hours later, Grandpa drove up in
a utility vehicle. He killed the engine and walked over to
me, where I lay in a heap on the ground. With great care,
he maneuvered himself into a seated position beside the
tree. He leaned against its trunk and pulled my head and
shoulders against his chest. He just held me there without
uttering a single word, kissing the top of my head and
smoothing my hair until the fireflies came out.

**Lesson 30: Loss comes in many forms; all those forms are
painful.**

Chapter 27

Whanged my
entire head. I was still dressed in my clothes from
yesterday. Dirt-covered, smelly, and snotty. My eyes
were nearly swollen shut, but the thin layer of sunlight
piercing the shades in the motel room still stung them. As
I pushed the quilt off me, I noticed a small body in bed
beside me. My grandma awoke with a start and grabbed
her chest for a moment.

"You scared me, girl," she said. "Are you feeling
better today, hon?"

*Am I okay? I don't even remember how I got back to my
bed.* The last thing I remembered was falling asleep on
Grandpa. Surely, he hadn't carried me. Grandma must
have read my mind through the darkness.

"You gave us quite a scare, Kincaid. When Joe came
by to check on you last night, I had to send him out to
find you and your grandpa. Joe carried you to bed while
you were still crying. I couldn't bear to leave you here by
yourself."

"I'm sorry, Grandma. I didn't mean to scare you."

She swung her legs over the side of the bed and stood
up carefully. In a few seconds, she opened the shades, the
light further invading my eyes. I covered my face with
my hands. She walked to my side and took me in her
arms.

"There, there, girl," she said. "You need hydration
and a good breakfast after a night of tears. Plus, that boy
of yours wouldn't leave, so he's camped out on my
couch."

"What about Aunt Sylvia?"

"She was asleep in Grandpa's recliner last time I saw her. Dane's driving in today."

My poor cousin. I couldn't imagine how he would feel when he found out about his father. And Sylvia was a wreck. I was a wreck and hadn't even known the man.

After Grandma left to make breakfast, I got up and took a quick shower and let cool water fall on my face before getting out. In the mirror, I was startled by how terrible I looked. I could almost hear Courtney standing behind me to tell me I looked like hell because I did. I wondered how much worse Aunt Sylvia must look and feel and wondered how long it would take Dane to come home to his mother. If he still considered this town his home—the previously unknown grave of the father he'd never known and never would.

When I was little, whenever I was mad at my mother, I'd wish Sylvia was my mother instead and Dane was my older brother. It was a fantasy I'd entertained often during the times when I missed my brother but couldn't recall a memory of him. I had plenty of memories of Dane.

As I sat in the chair beside the window to slip on my shoes, Joseph knocked on the connecting door and called out to me. I'd lost all of my embarrassment of looking terrible in front of him at that point. He entered with my permission and sat in the chair beside me. He didn't have to say anything; taking my hand in his was enough as he led me outside.

Hand in hand, we walked along the same trail I'd taken the night before, not speaking, just being together.

We passed three older couples slowly jogging in neon tracksuits they'd probably bought ten years earlier. They waved as they passed, keeping time with the woman in front—a white-haired force with a smile too wide for her face and a fanny pack that sagged onto one of her thick thighs.

When we reached the lake, Todd and Veronica were there, running sprints together across the sand. Joseph and I stayed back and observed them from a bench near the trail where we sat as if it were our planned destination.

"They're getting married, you know," Joseph said, gesturing toward Todd and Veronica. His voice cracked like he'd saved it up, waiting all night to talk to me. "They've decided not to wait. It'll be weird without her here."

"What'll you do? Do you have any other family?" I didn't know the state of my family yet and wasn't sure I had the right to ask about his.

"Not really any other family to speak of. Not good options, anyway. Dad was an only child, and Mom was estranged from her family. There was her great-uncle or cousin or someone out in Oregon or Washington, who she still spoke with when Veronica was little. He's so old there'd be no point in going that far."

"If Veronica leaves, you'll have to go with her, won't you?"

He shook his head. "I won't do that. The last thing a newlywed wants is her kid brother tagging along. I'll be fine. I've got a good case for emancipation, and if not…"

Emancipation. I only knew the term from books and movies when teenagers sued their abusive or drug-addicted parents for the right to live independently. "If not, then what? A group home? The foster system? That's not fair."

He laughed and turned to me. "Like any of this is fair? This whole year has been the worst and best in my whole life all wrapped into one, and it's just barely past the halfway point."

What more could I say?

"I'll be eighteen in two years anyway," he continued, turning a stone he'd picked up over and over in his hand. "A friend's parents would probably agree to be responsible for me until I finish school. I guess I can still live in my house when it's not a crime scene anymore, though I'm not sure I want to. Veronica doesn't want to go back there. She stayed at Sylvia's house last night. Sylvia mentioned letting me stay with her at one time, but I don't know if that's still possible with everything that's happened. She may want to get out of here and live closer to Dane."

"Makes me sound pretty stupid for worrying which of my parents I'll live with if they get divorced."

"That's not what I'm saying, Kincaid. My sucky things don't make yours suck less by comparison. Everything's going to be okay for both of us. It has to be. We've both dealt with enough already, damn it." He took my hand and kissed it before leaning his forehead against it. "Just promise me we'll always be friends, okay? Even if you decide to break up with me someday. We tragedy-magnets have to stick together."

"I promise. Always. And I don't really want to break up with you."

"Me neither. That was really terrible yesterday. Are you okay?"

I tucked myself under his arm. "I remembered something about my brother's death. I had forgotten I was there that day—the day he died. It's all so clear to me now, how much it broke my parents. It's not their fault. I think they really have tried to stay together for me, but as much as they love each other, the pain's poisoned them. After last night, I think I'm okay with them getting divorced. Maybe they have to. To heal, you know? Like they can't do it together because they're both too broken."

"And maybe everything will work out because they'll grow stronger where the scars fuse together." Joseph kissed my forehead. "At least, that's what Veronica's surgeon said about her broken bones. They're stronger where they've healed from the fractures."

Maybe it was true for everybody.

Lesson 31: Scars are not weaknesses—just proof of someone's strength.

Chapter 28

W hat I needed most was to talk to my best friend. I was relieved when Courtney answered on the first ring.

"Geez, Kincaid, that sounds awful," Courtney said after I'd described the events at Joseph's house.

I turned over on the motel bed and twisted the phone cord around my hand. "I don't know what Joseph will end up doing. He's staying at a friend's house until the police are done with their investigation. Who knows how long that'll take...murder and all?"

"I can't believe the dead guy was your uncle...or would have been, right?"

"Probably would've been. Aunt Sylvia loved him so much."

"Sounds like it." Courtney sighed into the phone. "What else are you not telling me?"

She always knew. I told her about the make-out session with Joseph and how it had ended. She gasped.

"Oh. My. God!"

I giggled, remembering the terrible movie from earlier in the summer. "It was so weird. I thought I'd done something wrong."

"Kincaid! I'm appalled!" She dissolved into giggles.

Maybe it was wrong to be laughing while Sylvia and Dane were in mourning, but I had to focus on something else to drive the sadness out of my mind. I was happy thinking about my relationship with Joseph until Courtney asked for news about my parents.

"I haven't talked to them in a few days. Not since all this happened. Grandma said Mom's coming here to talk to me at the end of the month."

"Just your mom?"

That was the problem. Dad wasn't coming with her, so in the pit of my stomach, I knew what the news would be. "Yeah. Just her. Dad has to get back home to work."

"Call me the minute you know something."

"Promise."

After Courtney hung up, I pulled out my notebook and wrote a letter to my parents.

Dear Mom and Dad,

I'm sorry for disappointing you earlier this year. I knew people like Derek were bad news, and I should have listened to you. I promise I'll do better at listening from now on.

Thank you for sending me to Grandma and Grandpa's place for the summer. I'd like to think you sent me here to learn a few things and not just to dump me off somewhere. Either way, I learned valuable lessons this summer.

I hope you both notice how much I've grown up this summer. With help from my favorite poet, Eduardo Martinez, I am just beginning to understand the loss you two went through with Patrick. I was there that day. I remember the physical show of your grief, and the memory alone broke my heart all over again. I imagine that happens for each of you all the time.

Patrick was your perfect child. I'll never be him, but if you'll let me, I promise I'll be the best Kincaid I can be. I want you to be proud of me. I want you to understand why I want to be an author, or at least support my decision. I want to capture all these emotions we have as people in a way that lets others

201

feel it in their chests when they read my work. I have a long way to go, but I think I can get there someday.

While I want you to stay together, I understand if you can't. Just please don't make me have to choose to only love one of you. I can't do that.

Your loving daughter,

Kincaid

With everything that had happened, my mom was anxious to get to me and to her sister as the end of July drew near. Sylvia was strong on the outside, but I could tell she was a wreck on the inside. Dane came home to be with his mother for a few days during a break from his summer program. There was a state police investigation into Mitch's death since it had been ruled a homicide, but any evidence had likely been washed away long ago. Sylvia said it was pretty much a cold case from the beginning.

Joseph and I were still in shock from what we'd found, but we tried to make the best out of the rest of our summer together. We went to see a few more movies, hung out with our friends, and caught a late summer dance recital with Heather and Kevin. I enjoyed every moment I spent kissing Joseph, holding his hand, and swimming with him in the lake. I missed my parents, but I dreaded the end of the summer. I didn't want my time with Joseph to end.

It was after lunch one day at the end of July when I went back to my room to wait on Mom's arrival. I stretched out on the bed with a book and attempted to read, but I couldn't keep my mind from wandering. After several failed attempts, I put the book on the nightstand and closed my eyes. I shouldn't have been nervous to see my own mother, but I was.

She was coming to tell me one of two things—either she and Dad were staying together or they weren't. Yes or no. Married or divorced. I only had a little while longer to know if their marriage would become another statistic.

The sound of a car door slamming woke me from a nap I hadn't known I needed. Mom's signature knocking came seconds later. I took a deep breath and walked over to my door. Before I could finish pulling open the door, Mom had her arms around me. I leaned against her and let her hug me until I could barely breathe, and my eyes filled with tears.

"Oh, my baby girl, I've missed you so much," she whispered into my hair.

"I've missed you, too, Mom; I can't breathe…"

She released me and grabbed my hand, pulling me out onto the small porch. "Let's walk while we chat."

Until we were in the middle of the walking trail, Mom said nothing. Neither did I. I desperately wanted to know my fate, as afraid of it as I was. No matter what she was about to tell me, I knew things were changing.

"I guess you're wondering what Dad and I have been doing these past few weeks."

"I'm still a little upset you didn't tell me what was going on before I came here, but I can't really do anything about that."

"That's fair," she said, motioning for me to sit with her on a bench. I walked over but remained standing in front of her with my arms crossed over my chest. "The marriage retreat came highly recommended by a pastor I started talking to last year."

I huffed. "Last year…" I wanted to forgive her for real like I thought I had already, but it was hard to hold back the hurt and anger I'd held in my heart for most of the summer.

"Dad and I just grew apart, Kincaid. It wasn't something either of us wanted; it just happens sometimes."

Happens sometimes? Like the fighting that had seemed to escalate when I got in trouble. "Is it my fault?"

"No."

I thought back and realized that even before my trouble, they'd stopped talking and laughing with each other—at least around me. They became silent in our car rides long before they drove me to the motel. "Because of Patrick?" I stared at the ground and wrote my initials in the dirt with the tip of my shoes.

"Patrick? But—"

"Patrick died because of me." A lump rose in my throat that was impossible to swallow. I tried to speak again but couldn't.

Mom got up and grabbed my shoulders. "How could you think that?"

"You said so yourself to your friend. Patrick died because my blood wasn't a match to his and he couldn't get the transplant. It's all my fault, and that's why Dad is always mad at me. You had me to save Patrick and I couldn't." It was all I could take. I broke down crying in my mother's arms.

I could feel Mom's chest heave against me as she led me back to the bench and held me. Her tears soaked into my scalp as she sobbed against my head. "Oh, baby, no. No, no, no, it wasn't your fault. It wasn't anybody's fault, but especially not yours. You were just a baby…my baby girl. I wanted you and your brother my whole life, Kincaid. I didn't have you to save Patrick; I had you to save me. Being your mother is the greatest gift I could have ever asked for."

"Mom…I'm sorry."

"Baby, I love you so much." She pushed me out of her lap to face her. "Look at me, Kincaid." I did, but it was excruciating to look at her tear-stained face. "Look at me and hear me right now. I was already pregnant with you when we found out Patrick was sick the first time. I promise you that. I was three months along when we got his diagnosis. I wanted you. Your father wanted you. When Patrick relapsed, he was so sick…well, losing him was devastating for your father and me, and you, too, I know. You were so little, but you idolized your brother."

"I did…"

Mom pulled me back into her arms. "I figured if I could survive losing him, I could survive anything," she said. "But I can't survive you blaming yourself for his death. You're part of the reason we had him as long as we did, Kincaid. He fought so hard to live for you, baby. Treatment after treatment. Remission and then that damn disease came back and took him away from all of us."

"I remember the day he died, Mom, it was scary, and I didn't know what to do."

"You were so young, not even five years old yet. But you want to know what Patrick's last coherent words were to me? He said, 'take care of my baby sister.' And your dad doesn't hate you. He could never hate you."

After we'd cried out what felt like a year's worth of tears, Mom told me what she and Dad had decided to do—a temporary separation. They still loved each other and didn't want to divorce but needed time apart to miss each other and work on their own issues with separate counselors. Part of the deal was that I would go see a counselor as well to cope with everything. I reluctantly agreed, not that I had a choice. I wasn't sure about talking to a stranger about my problems, but I realized that everyone was a stranger until you got to know them. Maybe it wouldn't be so bad to have an impartial opinion on all the things running through my head.

We went back to Grandma and Grandpa's apartment, and I sat in the living room as they discussed our next move, which would be happening before the new school year. Mom would need to secure another job, but she was certain she had a lead at a business in town. Dad would be moving separately after he secured the sale of our house and would find a place of his own somewhere nearby. They'd both agreed that leaving the house where Patrick had died would be good for our whole family. Until then, I would get to see Dad during school breaks and every other weekend. Even though Mom was insistent that it was not a divorce, it felt and sounded like one in all her explanations.

I wasn't sure how to feel as I excused myself to my room to call Courtney. I don't remember a single word she spoke on the phone after "hello" because we were both crying too hard, but I ended the call with a vague sense of us having promised to call each other all the time. Despite that, it felt like I was breaking up with my best friend and everything I'd ever known. At the same time, it was a relief to have the promise of a new start at a school where I already had a boyfriend and friends and where no one else knew about my expunged shoplifting record.

It was just before sunset when I walked to the lake to get away from everyone. Joseph had been away all day to deal with his own family stuff with Veronica. I missed him but figured I'd call him later to get his news.

Thinking back to the beginning of the summer, I could never have guessed how close Joseph and I would become. Things hadn't been the same between us since the discovery of Mitch's body in his backyard, and how could they? Grandpa was right; seeing a human skeleton changed people. I was changed. Life and love were more fragile than I'd ever realized before. Ed had taught me that. Remembering Patrick had solidified the lesson. And as for my parents, I already knew in my heart what I thought their outcome would be, and I was okay with my feeling that they would never reconcile.

I sat next to the closed lifeguard's tower and looked out on the darkening water. It wasn't the ocean, but it felt like it could lead me to the whole world if I could stop being afraid.

"I was wondering where you went," Joseph said as he sat next to me on the ground, startling me. By that time, it was dark. "I met your mom. She seems nice. She also told me you'd be moving here in a couple of weeks. I thought you could use someone to talk to, but I went to your room, and you weren't there."

"I just needed to get away for a bit, you know? I mean, I had already guessed what was coming, but I didn't realize how hard it would be to know for sure."

"I guess you're still pretty mad at both your parents."

"Sad more than mad. I was too little to understand what losing my brother did to them since I don't remember them before it happened. It's a little hard to stomach that love wasn't enough for them to stay together. Especially since they claim to still love each other now. Love should always be enough."

"Are you going to be okay?"

"I think so. Mom and I are moving in with Aunt Sylvia. She's lonely with Dane away at college, so it should be nice. And Dad is planning to leave his business under his manager's direction and take over for a plumber here who's planning to retire at the end of the year."

"At least you'll get to see them both a lot."

"I'm more excited about getting to go to school with you. I'll miss Courtney, though."

Joseph rubbed some dirt off my knee. "Maybe they'll get back together after the separation," he said. I shook my head as my eyes filled with tears again, which shouldn't have been possible, considering how much I'd cried earlier. "You don't think so?"

"No." I let Joseph put his arm around me, and I rested my head on his shoulder. "They're too broken. I finally understand that now. Love is too complicated. It's fragile and scary as hell."

Joseph held me as he rested against a tree, and we sat in silence as the lights beside the lifeguard stand started glowing. As much as I wasn't ready to go back and face my family, I eventually stood and offered Joseph my hand to help him up. He took it and looked up at me, and I wanted to stay in that moment a little longer.

Once on his feet, Joseph smiled at me with the shyest expression I'd ever seen from him. I couldn't help but blush as I returned his smile.

"Hey, Kincaid," he said.

Silence followed. "What is it?" I asked.

"Complicated or not," he muttered. "I think I love you."

More silence. Wishing for my first kiss over the summer had come true, but I never even considered wishing for someone to fall in love with me. Maybe it wasn't something to be wished for but to be prayed for.

"Hey, Joseph...complicated or not, I think I love you too."

If my life were a movie, that would have been the moment when Joseph and I kissed as the screen faded to black. Credits would roll as a romantic song softly hummed into the theater. In reality, I tripped over my own feet trying to hug him, and we both tumbled into the sand. After several minutes of much-needed laughter that didn't stop until both of our stomachs ached, we walked back to the motel hand in hand.

Lesson 32: First love is always the deepest and grabs you the hardest. The feelings last forever, even if they're only nostalgic. If you're lucky, that first love is your only love.

I thought I had everything all figured out long before I stayed at my grandparents' motel the summer I turned sixteen. Back when I was young and impressionable, I had no idea going in that I would learn more about life that summer than I could ever imagine.

I learned about flaws and forgiveness. I learned about unconditional love and loss. I learned that sometimes love isn't enough to make things work and learned that sometimes it is. Through it all, I learned that everything would be okay as long as I had people I could count on. One of the people I encountered that summer became the biggest influence on my adult life.

My grandparents are gone now. When I walk the grounds of the motel they called home during their golden years, my heart still aches for them. I expect to find them walking hand in hand on the trails, laughing at something only funny to the two of them. Sometimes, when I close my eyes, I can still hear their voices echoing off the trees surrounding the lake.

This whole place is mine now, and I run it with my wonderful husband, Joseph, although we don't live here at the motel. Our children are still young, so they'll get the benefit of seeing the place that helped me grow up if I can get their tablets out of their hands long enough to pay attention to the beauty that surrounds them.

ABOUT THE AUTHOR:

Brandi Easterling Collins grew up in Arkansas where she still resides with her husband, two children, and two dogs. When she's not writing or reading, she enjoys spending time with her family, thrift store shopping, painting, drawing, and leisurely walks outside.

What I Learned That Summer is her third novel. Her first novel, *Caroline's Lighthouse*, is a young adult paranormal mystery/romance. Her second novel, *Jordan's Sister*, is a new adult romance.

For more information, about future publications, visit caniscareyou.com.

www.ingramcontent.com/pod-product-compliance
Lightning Source LLC
Chambersburg PA
CBHW032119170626
46808CB00006B/2007